Hope Stanford

Down the Way

A Novel: Vol. I.

Hope Stanford

Down the Way
A Novel: Vol. I.

ISBN/EAN: 9783337045128

Printed in Europe, USA, Canada, Australia, Japan

Cover: Foto ©Andreas Hilbeck / pixelio.de

More available books at **www.hansebooks.com**

CONTENTS.

Vol. I.

———

DOWN THE WAY.

CHAPTER I.

THE HEART'S DESIRE.

LIKE many other men who, while possessing a large share of the good things of the world are yet disappointed of their heart's desire, Mr. Wedgwood Hilton's life was clouded by regret that he had no son to succeed him at Blithefield Manor.

The fine house, built in the best style of Queen Anne's days, stood in the midst of a well-timbered park, which had been in the possession of the Hiltons for nearly three

centuries; but the original Elizabethan
mansion had been burnt down by Cromwell's
soldiers, who, according to tradition, had not
been particular in inquiries for the safety
of its owner and his family, one at least of
whom had perished in the ruins, which fact,
coupled with a want of money, had caused
a lapse of sixty years between the destruc-
tion of the old house and the beginning of
the new. But since that time the Hiltons
had prospered. Careful management and
judicious marriages had restored the family
to more than its former wealth; and if the
present Mr. Hilton had possessed a son to
come after him, he would have been able to
leave him a rich man, even after giving
liberal portions to the five daughters whom
he regarded with mingled feelings of pride,
affection, and disappointment. He was anything but an indifferent father. When his
wife mourned over the birth of each suc-

cessive daughter, he would remark, with
cheerfulness: "The more the better, my
dear; we cannot have too many of them,
and can only hope for a variety next time."
But the fifth disappointment was too much
for Mrs. Hilton; she never held up her head
after it, but quietly grieved herself out of
the world when her youngest little girl was
five years old.

Mr. Hilton had no thought of marrying
again. To have had a son to succeed him
would have crowned his life, and left him
scarcely anything to desire; but as this
happiness had been denied him, he set to
work to make the best of it, and to educate
his eldest daughter for the position, as his
heiress, in which he intended to place her.
The younger girls should be treated with
justice and liberality, but they could not all
be eldest daughters, and they would have no
more right to complain at their sister being

put above them than if it had been the longed-for son.

There was one point on which Mr. Hilton was very decided. Should Adelaide marry contrary to his wishes, or should her husband refuse to take his name and live at Blithefield, there need be no difficulty, no quarrel; but the mantle would fall from her shoulders to fit itself, as best it could, to those of her next sister, who might, perhaps, find it easier to fulfil the required conditions; and if not—why, "Were there not five of them?" said Mr. Hilton, with a half-humorous shrug of his shoulders; and perhaps it might even come to the turn of little Erica in the end, and atone in some measure for the indifference of her mother, who had regarded her as the crowning drop in her cup of disappointment.

Adelaide was anxious to do her best to fit herself for her proposed position, and had no

doubt that when the time came for her to
marry, there would be no difficulty about the
conditions exacted by her father; but alas!
soon after she was twenty she gave her heart
away to the rector of a neighbouring parish,
who had not even the choice given him of
changing his name and renouncing his profession; for Mr. Hilton at once decided that
Adelaide must choose between her lover and
her inheritance, as he could not consent to a
clergyman as his successor, and had, besides,
a personal disinclination to the Reverend
Edgar Paget, whose soft manners, excellent
character, and handsome face, had won his
daughter's heart. He had nothing to say
against him; he was a most estimable man,
to whom any girl's welfare might safely be
trusted, but he could never be master at
Blithefield; and Adelaide, allowed to follow
her own wishes, retired contentedly to the
pretty country rectory, with ten thousand

pounds, and her sister Janet stepped into her place.

For a year or two all went smoothly. Janet was not so capable as her sister, nor such a good manager; but she was willing to learn, and thought a good deal more of her proud position than Adelaide had ever done, and even went so far as to attempt to stifle an affection for a handsome young officer when she found that her father did not care for his society. Janet was a good girl, but if Mr. Hilton could have had his way, he would, from the first, have passed her over and chosen her next sister, Edith, as his successor. It was, of course, an advantage that Janet should be so tractable while he was alive to watch over and direct her; but she would need more firmness of character when his death put the whole management of affairs into her hands, and when after a time he found that, with the best intentions, she still showed a lamentable incapacity for business, and a patient and hopeless devotion to Walter Bonar, he pleased both himself and her by asking her lover to the house, when he came home on leave, and at the end of three months gave her a gay wedding, and the same portion as her elder sister, and turned his attention towards the training of daughter number three.

It would be scarcely too much to say that for three or four years Edith Hilton had regarded her chance of being mistress of Blithefield as almost a certainty. Of stronger and earlier developed character than her sisters, she had clearly seen the points in which they and their chosen husbands had failed to meet her father's requirements, and had carefully and dutifully trained herself to avoid them. She knew that her sisters had failed—not only from a natural incapacity for management,

but because the life they were expected to lead
demanded too great a sacrifice of personal
and domestic ease and happiness; and she
resolved from the first that she would consider her own wishes of no account in comparison with the duties her high position
would force upon her, if she once made up
her mind to accept them, and on that point
she never felt a moment's hesitation. Her
elder brother-in-law, Mr. Paget, was amiable
and unworldly, and about as capable of
managing an estate as his second son, who
was still in long clothes at the time of her
promotion; Janet's husband, Captain Bonar,
was endued with more worldly wisdom, but
it had been misdirected; and fancying himself a good deal more knowing than he was,
he had let himself get mixed up with a
rather disreputable set of companions, whom
he had solemnly promised to renounce before
Mr. Hilton would consent to intrust his

daughter to him. But a man, however honest his reformation might be, who had a suspicion of a fancy for racing and betting, was not to be thought of as the master of Blithefield; and although Edith knew that her father would not have expressed to her a wish that she should remain unmarried, she knew that the only sort of person who would be welcome to him as a son-in-law would be a sober young member of Parliament with staunch Conservative views, or a country-loving younger son of one of the neighbouring noblemen, who would not at all despise a connection with the Hiltons, and Blithefield for a home.

It would be no great sacrifice, Edith thought, if she was called upon to deny herself the lot her sisters had chosen; many women were happy enough unmarried, even without such prospects as hers, and having reached twenty without even a passing flutter of the heart, she considered herself in little danger of the weakness—which at the same time she despised and admired—of losing her world for love. There was nothing hard or unamiable about her; she had no theories of woman's rights, and rather preferred the society of men; but she did think her sisters foolish, if not wrong, in so lightly throwing away the grand position, the power and influence, which might have been theirs, for the sake of the first wooers who came across their path, and who, while in no way unworthy, had nothing to distinguish them from the common herd.

There was every reason why—as heiress—she should marry, if her choice was a wise one. Even in his lifetime her father would prefer to have a son-in-law who would be capable of more comprehensive management than was in the power of any woman, however gifted or willing she might be; but the

one thing she dreaded was that a suitor
should present himself who should satisfy
her father and not herself, some one so excellent that she could not reasonably refuse
him, and who yet might fall far short of her
ideal, or take from her the power and
authority which was fast becoming, by an-
ticipation, like the breath of life to her.
She had no objection to a king for her
domain, but she must be the queen; it must
be a joint reign, or perhaps, unconfessed to
herself, she intended her husband to be only
royal consort, while she remained the sove-
reign ruler.

CHAPTER II.

A DISCORD.

As time went on Mr. Hilton found more and more reason to congratulate himself on the marriage of his elder daughters. They had always been affectionate, tractable, and anxious to please him ; but ability was wanting, and Edith's clear understanding enabled her to comprehend, almost at a glance, things which to the end of their lives would have been to them a hopeless puzzle. But glad as he was that these excellent and incapable children had chosen other paths for themselves, he rejoiced even more over the fact that there was no probability—at least at present—of the inheritance falling to the share of his fourth daughter, Laura. Rather giddy little Erica, who would never be anything but a butterfly, as mistress of Blithefield, than the cold, ill-tempered, unlovable girl whose otherwise aimless existence seemed spent in making those with whom she lived discontented with themselves, and dissatisfied with others.

The only plain one in a handsome family, and the only unpleasant one in a set remarkable for their amiability, Laura had from childhood been rather neglected.

" My dear," said an out-spoken governess, " no doubt you cannot make yourself either handsome or clever, but you *can* make yourself pleasant and useful, and therefore beloved; at present you are neither, and you only make yourself of importance by the power you possess of making us all uncomfortable." And this speech Laura remembered, and this power she prized. They might look down upon her as much as they pleased, they might despise her dulness, and pity her unattractive appearance; but she could make them feel, and she was not sparing of her power, until even her father felt the burden of her ill-temper and almost hated her, as a discord in the harmony of the household.

If Edith should by any means forfeit the inheritance, of a surety it should not go to Laura. It was his to do as he pleased with, and he would rather sell his cherished property than let it pass into her hands. Clever enough to detect and even imagine slights to herself, Laura had guessed her father's intentions; and if she had felt in need of an excuse for the discomfort she caused in the household, she would have considered this as amply sufficient. She did not particularly wish to be mistress of Blithefield—she knew that the management of the estate would be too difficult for her; but she hated the idea of Edith's being put so far above her, and would have rejoiced if she, like her sisters, had forfeited her place. She even felt capable of trying to influence her father against his dearly-loved daughter, of whom she felt a bitter jealousy; but she would probably only fail, and expose herself to his anger, and after all she would gain nothing by it herself. If Edith should make an unsuitable marriage, which was very unlikely, she felt sure that her father would strain many points to evade putting her into the important place, for which he had never taken the pains to make her in any way fitted.

Laura's bringing up had been in every way injudicious. Her plain face and uncomfortable temper had made the care of her a duty in which there was no satisfaction; and during several important years of her childhood she had been systematically neglected by her governesses, who, finding that this pupil could never be a credit to them, almost entirely passed her over after her mother's death; only gave her lessons when it was quite convenient, and allowed her to remain in a state of ignorance, which nothing but great and continued efforts on her own part in after-years could have counterbalanced, and these efforts she had no motive for making. She felt dull and ignorant, for her faculties had never been awakened; and as after a time it was taken for granted that it was a waste of labour to give her more than the plainest teaching, and that any accomplishment was beyond her reach, she learned to think the same herself, and made no attempt at improvement. There was one thing, however, in which she excelled, and to which she devoted the greater part of her time, and this was needlework—not of a kind that required originality, but which might be copied stitch by stitch; and over this she would sit by the hour together, seldom raising her eyes from her embroidery frame, and until Edith's promotion aroused her jealousy, being, in truth, as little interested as she seemed in what went on around her.

Being only a year younger than Edith, she was, of course, expected to join in her amusements, and go with her into society, and to this she made no objection; but the only time she seemed to derive pleasure from it was when she was given handsome materials, and allowed to make her own dress for some particular occasion; then she would shut herself up in her room, and without asking help or advice from any one, would appear at the proper time in a costume so perfect in fit and workmanship that even Edith regarded her with wonder and envy.

Laura's awakening to more active feeling happened soon after Janet's marriage. At a large party at a neighbour's house she was sitting as usual a little withdrawn from the rest of the company, watching them from the half-shelter of a curtain, when two ladies sat down near her, and not being aware of her presence, began to talk of her.

" I see Mr. Hilton has brought the ugly daughter out again; I really cannot understand his motive in doing it : she pleases no one, and never seems pleased herself," said Mrs. Cresset, a lady of whom Laura knew little.

" Well, poor girl ! " answered her companion, Mrs. Fowler, " of course they cannot very well keep her at home; I don't believe there is anything worse about her than a bad temper, and perhaps we should not think so much of that if Edith was not so very charming ; it does one good to see that girl with her father : she so fond and he so proud."

"Yes, it is fortunate for him that Edith comes first; he must have passed Laura over, she is neither clever nor good-hearted enough for such a position. I wonder if different training would have done anything for her."

"I fancy not much, she seemed hopeless from a child; and I have known them all their lives, you know. She was always what I should call spiteful, and she frightened me to-day by the look she gave out of her dull eyes when some one trod on her beautiful dress. I believe that is the only thing she cares for, oddly enough ! "

Then something else attracted the attention of the speakers, and Laura no longer cared to listen. She was not vexed by what she had heard—she was too well accustomed to being called ugly and ill-tempered to care about it; but her dislike of Edith swelled into a passion as she contrasted their two positions—neglect, coldness, and disfavour falling to her share, while Edith possessed beauty that no one could gainsay, talent— at least sufficient for her father's require- ments—and the love of every one who learned to know her.

Laura had no pride in Blithefield, and it would have given her little pain to see it pass into the hands of strangers; she felt like an alien from the family, and it would have been difficult to adjudge the portion of blame due to her and to others. No doubt the neglect shown towards her in her child- hood had soured her temper, but she had since had many opportunities of making her- self, if not beloved, at least regarded with

kindness as she grew older; for Adelaide
had been too indolently indulgent to cross
her in anything reasonable, and Janet, from
a sense of duty, had tried to befriend her
and bring her forward. Had the reign of
either lasted for a longer time the result
might have been different; but as it was,
they only succeeded in awakening in her
a one-sided interest in family affairs,
which roused her jealousy but not her
affection.

Nor were these sisters who had been kind
to her at home able to do anything for her
since they had married. Their husbands
detested her, for she generally contrived to
disturb them by allusions to their having
failed to satisfy her father's requirements, and
did not even scruple, with a kind of mocking
sympathy, to class them with herself as
victims to the favouritism shown to Edith.
Cheerfully as they had accepted their wives

and their portions, and excellent husbands as
they had proved themselves, they could not
but feel a pang of regret that beautiful
Blithefield was beyond their reach, especially
when they looked at their handsome boys,
whom they would have trained with strictest
care to fit them for the position of its master.
"Poor little fellows!" said Laura one day,
when they were playing with their grandfather and Erica on the lawn. "Who can
tell but that one of them would have been
the heir but for father's infatuation for
Edith?" Captain Bonar's face flushed as he
turned silently away, but Mr. Paget would
not let the occasion pass. "You are wrong
to make such a speech, Laura," he said
gravely; "there was never any thought of
Blithefield for us or for our children; nor
do we for a moment begrudge Edith the
position her good sense and good heart
fit her for so admirably; and you are

disrespectful in speaking of your father in such a manner."

"Yes, perhaps," answered Laura, coldly; "but I doubt if either you or Walter could deny that at that moment you were thinking that one of the boys ought to be master here."

Mr. Paget laughed uncomfortably, and hastily joined the merry group on the lawn; but placid Adelaide roused herself, and said: "What makes you say such disagreeable things? You have no business to speak to Edgar like that!"

But Laura only shrugged her shoulders, and went on with her work; and just then Edith, in a white dress, came out to join them, her face glowing with happiness at this family gathering; and with a shout of joy the little ones tumbled over each other to get to her, Erica ran and clasped her hand, and Captain Bonar involuntarily raised

his hat as a tribute to his sister-in-law, whom
he thought the noblest woman in the world;
but while every one else smiled upon her,
Laura's face grew pale with anger and
jealousy.

———————

CHAPTER III.

SONS-IN-LAW.

EASTER had fallen late, and the Blithefield woods were carpeted with primroses, when Mr. Hilton gathered a party of friends to his house to celebrate Edith's twenty-first birthday. He could not follow his inclination and make it a day of great rejoicing, for both Adelaide's and Janet's majority had been only quietly honoured; and although in his own heart he considered this daughter incomparably superior to them and to everyone else, it would not do to let all the world into the secret. He was therefore obliged to content himself with making only three or four additions to the party who had assembled on former occasions, and was disappointed of the company of his elder daughters and their husbands; Janet being kept at home by a new baby, and Adelaide by the recent death of Mr. Paget's father.

"I believe it is just as well that we are not going to be there," said Adelaide to her husband; "for although I am sure that none of us begrudge Edith her position, fallen nature does give a sigh now and then at the thought of our beautiful boys."

"Yes, yes, my dear, it is natural for a mother; but the thought must be checked."

"Of course, Edgar! I don't often let it come uppermost, and should never think of mentioning it except to you; but I am sure Walter Bonar thinks a great deal more about it than I do, especially since last summer, when that uncomfortable Laura put it so

plainly before him; she saw the effect, and
often since has made opportunities for saying
the same sort of thing."

"That girl's perverted nature is one of
the saddest things I know," said Mr. Paget
sighing. "I am often strongly moved to
tell her how unchristian and unbearable her
conduct is; but she is careful to avoid giving
me a chance, and leaves me at the first
word."

"Yes, I have noticed that, and now for
some reason she includes me in her general
dislike, although when I was at home I
could get on pretty well with her; but her
manner to us is almost pleasant in comparison
with what it is to Edith. I declare sometimes it makes me shudder to see the bitter
dislike she has for her, and I could almost
believe she would be glad to do her an
injury."

"I hope it is not so bad as that, dear; but

if jealous feelings are fostered it is, indeed, hard to say where they will end."

But while the Pagets consoled themselves as best they might for their lost share in the Blithefield festivities, the Bonars were not so easily satisfied. Janet's second boy was no doubt a splendid little fellow, but he was a great inconvenience just then, for there were old friends assembled at her father's house whom she seldom had a chance of meeting, and it would also have been interesting to see Edith doing the honours for the first time to so large a party. She had never been tormented by the vague envy which troubled her husband, and would have simply enjoyed herself without any uncomfortable longings; but with him it was different, and although he well knew that he and his children had not even a remote chance of succeeding to Blithefield in the natural course of things, he could not—strive as he would and did—altogether check the thought that by marriage or some other means, the sisters might, one after another, fail to satisfy their father's requirements, and that the estate might one day be in the market, and within the compass of a very considerable fortune which he expected to inherit from a relative at some future time.

No one, he thought, could reign more worthily than Edith, he felt for her the heartiest brotherly affection, was proud of her beauty, her abilities, and the charm of manner and disposition which made her everywhere a favourite, but he scarcely felt as if he could be cordial to her possible husband. He had been perfectly well aware when he married that he knew nothing about the management of property, but he would have willingly and easily learnt all that was required, and he felt a little sore at every one's taking it for granted that he was unfitted for it. He could understand it well enough in the case of Edgar Paget: he was a clergyman to the backbone, he could never have given up his profession and devoted himself to worldly concerns, it would have been almost a mockery to ask him; but their two cases were very different, and it would have been a satisfaction to him through all his life if he had had the chance of refusing for himself his wife's possible inheritance. Even now, when the thought came, and could not always be driven away, that Blithefield might some day be for sale, it was not for himself that he looked forward, but for his son, his first-born, curly-headed darling, who, good husband as he was, absorbed three-quarters of his heart. And yet in spite of these uncomfortable and unmanageable feelings, he hankered after the festivities of Blithefield, and thought that, as Janet was getting on perfectly well and did not want him in the least, he might have been kindly urged to join the party.

" I see no reason why you should not ride over some time, Walter, and see what they are all about," said his wife; and he said he would do so, wishing at the same time that she had suggested that she could comfortably spare him for a day or two. But even if she had it was probable that the invitation to stay would not be given; Mr. Hilton would think it was his duty to be at home; and Edith, knowing him to be a fond husband and father, could not have thought of suggesting that he should remain.

Daisy Lodge—where the Bonars lived— for Walter had left the army when he married—was six miles from Blithefield, just outside the country town of Mornington. It was a pleasant little old-fashioned house,

covered with verandahs and creepers, and
had a good-sized garden, in which Captain
Bonar worked indefatigably, and which gave
him his chief occupation, besides his daily
ride on the handsome horse which had been
his father-in-law's wedding present. The
Bonars were comfortably off, and being so
nearly connected with Blithefield, were people
of some consequence in the neighbourhood,
although they went little into society, and
preferred living quietly; but Janet never, if
she could help it, refused an invitation from
her father, and was much vexed at being
unable to take her share in the present
festivities.

"Do ride over, Walter, and see what they
are doing," she said, the day after the
guests were expected. "And you might
ask Mrs. Mathewson to come and see baby
this afternoon. I am sure Edith will hardly
know what to do with an old lady; so it

will be quite a kindness to her, and I should not at all mind your leaving me if you care to dine there—indeed, I should like it, for you could tell me all about it afterwards."

"Oh, I scarcely think I shall do that!" said Captain Bonar; but he was pleased with the idea, and with her for suggesting it, and rewarded her by pretending to admire the ugly little three-days-old baby, who was, she assured him, the very image of himself. "And I should not be surprised if he was even handsomer than Phil," she said; "for I am afraid Phil's nose will never be a good shape, and I can see already that baby's will be just like yours." An insult which her husband could scarcely resent, and so passed over in judicious silence.

"So you really wish me, dear, to go and give messages to Edith and your aunt," he said diplomatically, and being assured that this was the case, he followed his own inclination, and set off with an easy conscience.

———————

CHAPTER IV.

OFFSHOOTS.

THERE was one guest at Blithefield who, without being aware of it herself, had been brought there for a special purpose. Mary Verney—a girl about Edith's age—was an orphan, with a small fortune of her own, enough to keep her from the necessity of earning her living, but not enough to enable her to live independently. Her aunt, Mrs. Mathewson, in whose care she had been placed, was a cousin of Mr. Hilton's, and had been a good friend and wise counsellor to him since his wife's death. She had encouraged Adelaide and Janet in making the happy marriages for which they were so much

better suited than for the position for which
they had endeavoured to fit themselves; she
had pointed out to him the parts of Edith's
character to the development of which she
thought his attention ought to be specially
directed, and she had proved to be right;
she had advised him to send Erica to school,
and had so relieved Edith from the difficulty
of having in the house a governess older and
wiser than herself, and yet to whom she
could no longer defer; and now finding how
hopelessly unamiable and unhelpful Laura
continued to be, she had persuaded him to
ask her niece Mary Verney to the house for
an indefinite visit, to be a companion to
Edith and to go with her into society, where
Laura's presence was more pain than pleasure
to herself and others. But in bringing Mary
to Blithefield just then Mrs. Mathewson had
a double object. She wished to persuade
Mr. Hilton to spare his dearly-loved daughter

to her for a while, and she thought that Mary's company would make the house endurable to him in her absence, which it certainly would not be with only Laura for a companion. Mary was bright, and cheerful, and unassuming, and Mr. Hilton, who had known her from a child, was disposed to think would be a pleasant addition to the family at any rate until Erica, who was now sixteen, was old enough to take her place at home; but it was understood that none of the girls should be told of the proposed arrangement until they were all better acquainted, but that Mary should simply be left behind for a long visit, until they saw how matters turned out.

Mrs. Mathewson had set her heart on taking Edith with her to London for two months, and giving her the advantage of glimpses into a wider world than was to be seen at Blithefield. It was not to be ex-

pected that she would learn much in so short
a time, but she would at least see that a
country neighbourhood, however admirable,
did not embrace everything that was good
in the world; and her standard of qualifi-
cations for her husband and the future master
of Blithefield must necessarily be raised, by
meeting other people who were well worth
knowing, and who were able to combine
mental culture with a practical knowledge of
the management of a rather difficult estate.
There were two types of men of whom Mrs.
Mathewson had a horror, and to one of these
she feared that Edith would fall a victim,
unless she should be made acquainted with a
variety of excellencies.

Of the Eton and Oxford bred sons of
country gentlemen there were several in
the neighbourhood of Blithefield, who were,
no doubt, well-principled, intelligent, and
unaffected, but narrow, and as it seemed

intentionally so, *their* hunters, *their* game preserves, *their* cricket clubs and county meetings formed their world, and as they were now they would be to the end of their days; and should one of them marry a woman whose aims were somewhat wider, who wished to combine the virtues of the country with the intelligence of the town, there would surely be discord and collision in the house. The second type, although less commonly to be met with, was even more to be feared,—the young parliamentary prig, a son perhaps of some noble family, who would talk and think a great deal of his duties, would take his wife away from home for several months in the year, would manage the estate by his own theories and despise her practical knowledge, and would be quite incapable of the hearty, kindly, wholesome intercourse which Mr. Hilton held with all those connected with him, and which seemed to have come by nature to those of his children who resembled him, and to Edith most of all.

Mrs. Mathewson had no wish to undertake the responsibility of finding a husband for her; she would be quite contented with teaching her whom to avoid; and she would have been far better pleased if she could have persuaded Mr. Hilton to accompany his daughter to London, and have thus enlarged his views also. But this she knew was impossible, and she was obliged to be satisfied with his promise, given very unwillingly on the first evening of her arrival, that if Edith seemed anxious to go he would do nothing to prevent her.

Besides Mary Verney, Mrs. Mathewson had brought with her to Blithefield a nephew, whose home had lately been broken up, and who was for the present in want of everything, occupation, interests, and, not least, money, wherewith to give himself a start in life. It was not altogether Geoffrey Poland's own fault that at twenty-eight he found himself in this condition, for he had been forced into a life he hated, in a Government office, by his father, just when he had set his heart on going to Oxford, and, fresh from a rather brilliant career at Marlborough, had a good chance of distinguishing himself. At the end of three years his father died, leaving him a few thousand pounds, and seeing no prospect of getting on in the position which had been chosen for him, he threw it up, followed his own inclination, and went through Oxford with credit, but with none of the distinction which he might have gained a few years before, and then found that he had nothing in the world to do with himself. He could not afford to be idle, and yet had no inclination or special aptitude for any profession; he would be

ashamed to continue long doing nothing,
but for awhile it was pleasant enough,
especially as his aunt, Mrs. Mathewson,
was delighted to give him a home, and he
could always quiet his scruples by deciding
that at some not very distant time he would
go abroad, and find that indefinite " something to do " in which so many seem to
implicitly believe.

Geoffrey was not altogether an agreeable
man, he was inclined to be self-absorbed
and dogmatic; but his aunt understood him,
and having no other near relations, he gave
to her all the affection which might have
been bestowed on a mother and sisters.   He
was a handsome man, but scarcely pleasing;
his distasteful work had given him a look of
discontent, and being several years older
than most men of his standing at Oxford, he
had kept to himself, and grown reserved
and melancholy.   About a month before the

visit to Blithefield, his peace had been disturbed by Mary Verney's coming to stay with her aunt for an indefinite time. He had never been accustomed to girls, and did not like them; and being unsettled and vaguely unhappy, Mary's cheerfulness—which Mrs. Mathewson had hoped would have a good effect upon him—was, instead, a constant jar; and longing for quiet, and having a fancy just then for trying what he could do in the way of literary work, he shut himself up in his aunt's library, and seldom appeared except at meal times.

Mary, who was simple and natural, and all her life had been popular with every one, had begun by cordially claiming cousinship, and demanding his interest in her pursuits; but he had responded so coldly that she was offended, and, being quick-tempered, did not attempt to conceal that she disliked and even in some measure despised him; for to

her energetic mind he seemed to be wasting
the best years of his life, and indulging
in unpardonable indolence, in taking so much
time for consideration before making a fresh
start.

It was not, therefore, entirely from
disinterested motives that Mrs. Mathewson
urged upon Mr. Hilton the advantage of
having Mary at Blithefield. Geoffrey was
far dearer to her than her niece could ever
be, and the longer he stayed with her the
better she would be pleased; but she knew
that the discordant element in the house
would soon drive him away, and she determined that it should be removed, if it could
be managed without injustice to Mary.

Geoffrey had been unwilling to go to
Blithefield; but his aunt strongly wished it,
and it was so seldom that she asked anything from him, that he could not refuse,
especially as he had serious thoughts of

leaving her as soon as they returned, and going for a few months' travel, to see if new scenes and new companions would suggest the hitherto unfound niche into which he could fit himself for the remainder of his life.

CHAPTER V.

FIRST COMPANIONSHIP.

THE party whom Captain Bonar found assembled at luncheon in the large hall at Blithefield, which they used for every meal excepting dinner, consisted, besides Mrs. Mathewson and her nephew and niece, of five or six people, all of whom were relations; but, as Mr. Hilton said, they were particularly fortunate in their relations, and he had brought up his girls to look upon their cousins as supplementary brothers and sisters.

There was one amongst them whom everybody liked, and who was treated by the whole family with indulgent kindness.

He had bestowed his affections on each reigning sister in turn, but did not consider himself mercenary in so doing; it was only a sort of worship of the highest, and the position of the mistress of Blithefield did seem to him very high, and he longed to win her, although if he had done so he would have been much embarrassed. His sliding scale of devotion was a great joke in the Hilton family; but Peter was quite inoffensive, and even Captain Bonar, who guarded his young sisters-in-law as jealously as if he had been really their brother, could not look upon his attentions as impertinent.

Peter had fully determined to make an offer to Edith during this visit: he was not going to let a prize escape him for want of asking for it, and every one in the house— Edith included—guessed his intention, and was amused by it. He was an idle man, but had quite enough to live comfortably

upon, and was a favourite amongst his relations, especially with Erica, who, just as
Walter entered the hall, sent the whole
party into a roar of laughter by saying, with
gravity and apparent innocence: "Whatever you do, Cousin Peter, please, don't
make me an offer when I am grown up, for
I should be quite certain to say Yes," and
Peter answered with equal gravity:

"No, my dear, I don't think you need be
alarmed; you would always be too flighty
to suit me, even when weighted with addi-
tional years and wisdom!"

And then Erica stopped her brother-in-
law in his progress round the table to give
him a kiss, and introduce him to Mary
Verney.

The other members of the company were
not particularly interesting. There were the
Wedgwoods, a self-absorbed young married
couple; Rachel Allen and her barrister

brother and two Misses Hamilton, none of whom had ever missed being present at weddings or other festivities at Blithefield; and an old Colonel Arnold, just come back from India, completed the party.

"Very glad to see you, Bonar!" said Mr. Hilton, heartily, "and doubly so, as your coming means good news of Janet."

"Yes, she is very well, and it was she who sent me. She wants you, Mrs. Mathewson, and any other baby-worshippers of the company, to go and see her new plaything."

"Poor Janet! It was good of her to give an excuse for your coming; but I daresay she did not much like it," said Laura, disagreeably.

"Why not?" asked Peter, wonderingly; but no one else thought of noticing Laura's speeches.

"I was longing for an invitation, Walter,"

said Mrs. Mathewson, pleasantly. "I have not seen Janet since her wedding-day; but she has written me many a letter in praise of Daisy Lodge, and I long to see it and her; and to tell you the truth, I so fully expect to be asked to be godmother, that I have got the christening cup already in my trunk."

"I do believe, Aunt Sarah, you would be godmother to all the world if you could," said Erica, laughing, "and give it—them —silver cups! O, Peter, which is right? my grammar *will* get mixed sometimes."

"Well!" answered Peter slowly, "you see, it all depends on the sense in which you use the word. If you mean to take the world as an aggregate of individuals"—but here he was interrupted by a general shout of laughter, and one excellent thing about him was, that he did not mind being laughed at; and when Erica patted him on the back and cried, "Bravo, Peter!" he was quite satisfied; for he wished to be amusing, and often found that he was so, although he was seldom quite sure how he had managed it. The only two grave faces at the table were Laura's and Geoffrey Poland's. Laura seldom laughed, certainly not at Peter, whom she detested; for he had a way of saying with apparent simplicity very cutting things about her unpleasant manner, and would sometimes stare at her as if she was something incomprehensible when she gave an ill-tempered answer to her father or sisters. As for Geoffrey, he was altogether in a bad humour that day. His aunt had talked to him a great deal of Edith, of her good looks, good disposition, and earnest endeavour to please and satisfy her father, until he felt convinced that this paragon, like all others, must be odious, and had determined beforehand to avoid her as far as possible; but

almost immediately he had been obliged to
confess to himself that his gracious young
hostess had not been over-rated. He could
not wonder that most people were fascinated;
but then he was glad to say, he was not like
most people, and he rather disliked her the
more for having upset his preconceived idea.
No doubt she was a very good sort of girl,
just of the kind to be popular, but for
himself he should prefer that pale, quiet
sister, who, unamiable as she appeared, had
probably a great deal more in her than the
rest of the family put together. So, to the
surprise of every one, and not least of Laura
herself, he gave the chief part of his attention to her; not that he found her agreeable,
but that it suited his humour to go contrary
to other people; and having given way to
his aunt's wishes by coming to Blithefield,
he thought he had done all that could be
expected of him, and was not bound to be

more sociable than he chose. Mrs. Mathewson was rather amused than amazed by his
contrariety; it was much more convenient
than if he had taken it into his head to
develop a hopeless passion for Edith, and
it was a good thing to have Laura's attention occupied, so that she had little time for
making herself unpleasant.

Before Walter had been in the room ten
minutes, Mr. Hilton resolved to take a
mean advantage of him, and throw upon
his shoulders the burden of entertaining this
somewhat difficult guest, who having hurt
his hand was unable to join the rest of the
party at tennis, and was not at all easy to
dispose of. The offer of a sort of general
stroll round had been refused in the morning,
but Geoffrey had afterwards become somewhat ashamed of betraying his ill-humour,
and at the beginning of luncheon had
civilly begged to be allowed to accompany

his host in his afternoon ramble. But although Mr. Hilton had agreed, he was still offended, felt no inclination for the society of this "young weather-cock," and congratulated himself not a little on his bright idea of making his son-in-law take his place.

"Poland was going to stroll with me through the oak wood this afternoon, Bonar," he said; "but I remember that I have letters to write, and will ask you to be my representative; you might take a look at the clearing we made in the autumn, and see how you think it looks, now that the timber has been taken away."

"I have just promised Erica to be her partner at tennis," answered Walter reluctantly; "but, of course, the match can stand over until another day."

"If Mr. Poland only wants a guide, I can offer my services," said Laura, quietly. "I am going to the lodge for my embroidery silks, which the carrier was to leave there last night."

At least half the people at the table looked at Laura, in amazement at her offering to do anything for anybody; but although she was quite conscious of their surprise, she took no notice, and Geoffrey hastened to assure her that he should be delighted to accompany her; not that this was at all true, for he could not persuade himself that he liked her society; but if Mr. Hilton did not choose to go with him, he certainly would not be bored with the company of that "self-conceited puppy" over whom Edith and Erica were making such a fuss; for although Walter did not deserve that description, he was rather too particular about his clothes and moustache, and would have looked the better for a little neglect; but he was a handsome man, and knew it, and took a pleasure in his good looks, while Geoffrey went almost too far the other way, and did not condescend to soften the ruggedness of his clever, hard-featured face, by either beard or moustache, although his aunt had persistently endeavoured to persuade him to it.

But although Geoffrey appeared satisfied at the prospect of the walk, Edith, knowing what an unpleasant companion Laura generally contrived to make herself, felt bound to interfere.

"Would you not rather drive with some of our party to Mornington to-day, Mr. Poland, and wait for the walk until to-morrow, when father could go with you?" she said, not meaning to vex her sister, but to provide due entertainment for her guest.

But although Geoffrey would have much preferred the drive he could not well refuse Laura's offer, and half an hour later lounged through the park by her side, at least enjoying the April sunshine.

"I hope you will light your pipe, Mr. Poland," said Laura, after rather a long silence, which succeeded their first remarks on the beauty of the day. "I am not at all accustomed to the consideration you might show to Edith or to any other lady, and should not object to it at all."

Geoffrey took advantage of this somewhat ungracious permission, and then felt bound to try to be agreeable.

"What a pride you must all take in this beautiful place!" he said. "It has been in your family for hundreds of years, has it not?"

"Yes; and no doubt all the others are proud of it, as you say; but I scarcely feel as if I had a right to share in their feeling."

" Indeed ? "

" Why, you see, I know that father would never give the place to me. With the others it has been different, they have all, except Erica, had their chance ; but, of course, I know that I have none."

" Why not ? " asked Geoffrey, in surprise.

" My father has done nothing to fit me for the position, and I could not fill it. He——well—I will say—he is not proud of me as he is of the others, and if it could be possible for Edith to displease him, I feel sure that he would make my incapacity an excuse for passing me over ; he has Erica to fall back upon, and she is being well educated."

Of course, Geoffrey could not know how distorted and unfair this account of matters was, and felt that he had no business to be receiving such a confidence at all ; but Laura had no intention of changing the subject just yet, and went on—

" I daresay, being a sort of connection, you have heard all about it—that my father means to give Blithefield to the first of his daughters who marries to please him, and I am sure that Edith will do that somehow; but I think it is very unfair on my brothers-in-law that they should both have been passed over because she was always my father's favourite."

This was very embarrassing, and Geoffrey tried to change the subject by suddenly pointing to a splendid cock pheasant which was sunning his gorgeous plumage a few yards from them ; but Laura just glanced at him, and returned to her subject.

" If I were Edith I should be almost ashamed to see Edgar and Walter, and still more my sisters ; but fortunately for her she does not feel it in that way."

"Fortunately, indeed!" said Geoffrey, "especially as she can be in no way to blame. Now, Miss Hilton, is that the lodge we are bound for, down there amongst the trees?" and then he contrived by asking many questions to avoid further confidences for the time. But when they had reached the lodge, and turned homewards again, he found himself at a loss for conversation, and Laura took advantage of it.

"What a terrible misfortune it is that we have no brother!" she exclaimed, as her companion expressed his admiration for the splendid oak woods which stretched away on either side. "It is such a dreadful idea that a stranger may some day be master here. I do think that if Edith is to inherit Blithefield she ought to remain unmarried!"

"I am afraid that is rather short-sighted," answered Geoffrey, laughing; "the difficulty would only be removed one generation ; she must leave it to some one."

"Of course, but perhaps none of us would be alive to see it pass into a stranger's hands." Laura was surprised at herself for this newly developed pride in Blithefield, which certainly in general she was far from feeling ; but that day it had fallen to her share for the first time to exhibit its beauties to an appreciative new-comer, and it had awakened in her a passing—but for the moment genuine—enthusiasm, which aroused great pity for her in Geoffrey's mind ; for although he thought her unattractive, and could see that she was unamiable, he also saw that she was neglected, and did not know that it was from her own fault, and that from most people she would have rejected kindness almost as an insult. But with him it was different, he had not attempted to be kind, he had simply talked to her apparently because she wished it, and she was not clear-sighted enough to detect the perverse ill-humour which led him for the time to thwart even his own inclinations.

After all, he thought, if it was a relief to this poor lonely girl to tell him her grievances it did not much matter to any one, he would never betray her confidences; so he let her talk on, until by the end of their walk he knew nearly as much of the history of the Hilton family as there was to know; but he reserved to himself the right of judging their characters from his own observation, rather than from Laura's warped and unloving descriptions.

"I do not think I have ever had a long talk in my life before," she said pathetically, turning round on the door-steps to look at her companion, with more gentleness than her face had often worn; and Geoffrey resolved that he would be kind to her during the few days of his visit, and was sufficiently interested in her to intend, if possible, to find out the reason for the general disfavour with which she was regarded.

———————

CHAPTER VI.

IN EDITH'S HONOUR.

ALTHOUGH Mr. Hilton had contrived to avoid the task of entertaining his uncongenial guest, the letters which had furnished him with an excuse made but little progress, and as soon as Mrs. Mathewson returned from her visit to Mrs. Bonar, he sought her out and settled down to a long talk with her.

"Well, Sarah," he began, "may I inquire what you hope to do in the end with that surly nephew of yours?"

"Not that, Wedgwood! Not surly."

"Well, perhaps, I should not have used the word; your—um!—unsociable nephew: will that do?"

"Has he ever been uncivil to you?" asked Mrs. Mathewson, with some resentment.

"Not exactly, but several times since he came yesterday he has made me feel that although I *am* his host, he would rather be without my company. No, he has never been uncivil—I could not say that, Sarah; but his patience, when I have been talking of subjects which interest me, has been *too* studied, and he is as yet perhaps too young a man to realise that affected interest in an old man's crotchets is, if detected, almost an insult. I do not doubt he means well, but he takes little pains to conceal that he considers the theories of the rising generation of infinitely more value than the careful and practical experience of a man of more than double his age."

"Surely, Wedgwood, you must have misunderstood him! He *has* strong opinions, and is rather obstinate in maintaining them, that I will not deny ; but I do not believe he ever intended, at least openly, to set his judgment before yours.   Poor boy ! his life has been sadly mismanaged, and if now that he is left entirely to his own guidance he goes rather into extremes, who can wonder, or blame ? "

" No, no, I do not blame—at least, not much.   I respect a young fellow who has the courage to uphold strong and disagreeable convictions ; I only say that his manner might be pleasanter.   I have seen Edith open her eyes in astonishment more than once when he has not taken the pains to conceal his contempt for some of my old-world notions."

" Wedgwood, you are accusing my nephew of failing to be a gentleman ! "

" No, I do not mean that.   I have little doubt that his manner would be tolerated or even approved by most particular people, of a sort, nowadays; but I only say it does not suit my ideas of courtesy. At luncheon, when Edith ask him to join the driving party, he refused more curtly than I thought fitting in speaking to a lady; but at least I shall have the comfort of knowing that while she is staying with you, no love-making will go on from that quarter, and shall have no misgivings in trusting her to your wise and kind keeping."

"Yes, I think you may be easy on that point," answered Mrs. Mathewson, laughing. "I confess that Geoffrey is a little beyond my comprehension. Why, with a housefull of pleasant, attractive girls he should devote nearly all his attention to Laura *is* odd; but I never saw the poor child so amiable to any one before, and one only wishes she would be the same to the rest of the household."

" It would be an uncommonly good thing for us all if she and Poland took a fancy to each other," said Mr. Hilton, who in general hated the idea of matchmaking, but had suffered too much from Laura's temper not to be eager to place her in the safe keeping of some one else.

" Well, I scarcely think I should be satisfied for Geoffrey," answered Mrs. Mathewson; " you know I think a great deal of him, and could not wish him to marry a girl who contrives to make even her own family anxious to get rid of her."

" Her ten thousand pounds would be worth his having," suggested Mr. Hilton.

" Wedgwood, I am astonished at you! I don't know you to-day! If you thought Geoffrey could marry her for that, I can scarcely imagine you would be willing to trust her in his hands."

" No, no, of course not; but sometimes

'our domestic cross'—as Paget calls her—is difficult to bear with, and my poor Edith has suffered sadly from her temper lately."

"Well—one can forgive her for feeling considerable envy of her fortunate sister—beauty, riches, and her father's love, which for all we know might be a precious posses-sion to her if she could ever gain it."

Mr. Hilton looked uncomfortable. " Of course, I do love the child in a certain way, I would do anything for her good; but even you, Sarah, can hardly call her lovable."

"No, and so you cannot wonder that I am not particularly anxious that she should fall to Geoffrey's share; but here they come up the avenue, and I suppose it is time for Edith to give us some tea."

There was to be a large dinner party at Blithefield that evening, and no one would have been either surprised or annoyed if, as had often happened before, Laura had refused to appear. In all unimportant matters she was allowed, for the sake of peace, to take her own way unquestioned; but Edith was anxious that her sister should not hold herself aloof on this occasion, and went to her room before dinner to try all her arts of persuasion if she found it necessary; but to her surprise she found Laura ready dressed, and was almost startled at the effect which a little well-chosen adornment had made in her appearance. Her dress of pale green, which had been chosen for a garden party the year before, was almost severely simple, but, being made by her own hands, suited her to perfection. and was trimmed here and there with bunches of delicate geraniums, exactly matching the pale pink coral ornaments which had fallen to her share from her mother's jewel case.

"My dear Laura! what have you done to yourself? you look perfectly lovely!"

exclaimed Edith in amazement; "I never saw you with such a colour in your cheeks, or dressed with such care. Is it all to do honour to my birthday?"

Laura laughed a little awkwardly. "Yes, that is just it," she said; "I supposed you would like me to look as well as I could, and as neither you nor father offered me a new dress, I made the best I could of this."

Edith felt a pang of self-reproach. It was an undoubted fact that she did neglect Laura; but then she courted neglect.

"My dear child!" she exclaimed, "if we had thought that you would join in any of the parties, you would have had just the same dresses as I have."

"No, no, Edith! stick to facts! _I_ am not the heiress: what does it matter how _I_ am dressed?"

"I confess it makes a difference," answered

Edith, candidly and with dignity; " but you would have had the same as Erica."

" The schoolgirl! Thank you! I think I prefer my own scarcity to that!"

" Really, Laura, you are very difficult to understand. If father had given you the most beautiful dress in the world, you would have managed somehow to make him feel that he was insulting you; but I must make haste down now—will you come with me?"

"No, thank you, I have no fancy for humbly following after the sun."

" A good thing for the sun on this occasion, for it might be eclipsed," answered Edith good temperedly, and then ran down stairs, fervently wishing that it was possible to do even her duty to Laura.

The dinner party was large, and somewhat dull, and was intended chiefly to show attention to those of the neighbours who would not care to be present at the dance on

the following evening, which was the chief
event to Edith and her younger visitors. It
was the first time she had been called upon
to entertain so large a party, and a consciousness of attention, and perhaps criticism,
brought a flush to her cheeks, although she
showed no other sign of nervousness, and
filled her place with dignity. Her father
watched her with undisguised pride, and
even Geoffrey was obliged to acknowledge
to himself that he could scarcely find a fault
in the manner of the young mistress of
Blithefield; but there was no doubt that
her beauty was greatly overrated, and he
did not himself admire the mixture of very
dark hair and large, light grey eyes, which
no one had ever thought of calling blue.

"Do you not feel proud of our cousin
to-night, Mr. Poland?" asked Rachel Allen,
one of the guests staying in the house, by
whom Geoffrey was seated at dinner.

"I think your cousin suits her place very well," he answered languidly.

"*Our* cousin—I suppose she *is* yours as well as mine."

"I don't know, I am sure; I never thought of claiming the relationship."

"Detestable man!" thought Rachel, who in common with the rest of the girls in the house, had taken a strong dislike to him, and had only consented to go in to dinner with him to please Edith, who had found difficulty in arranging the guests. "Of course she always fills her place well," she went on aloud, "but to-night she does more. I think her manner is simply perfect, so natural and dignified, although she must feel frightened to death."

"For what reason?" asked Geoffrey, looking with some interest at this warm partisan.

"Why, of course, at entertaining so many

people for the first time, and knowing that every one is thinking of her and noticing her."

"Is every one?"

"Of course! We have all of us only come to do her honour."

"I cannot say I had thought of it in that light. I knew Miss Hilton's birthday was the pretext for this gathering; but I imagined that any other would have done as well."

"Really, Mr. Poland, that is almost incredible; I think you wish to differ from us all, and I believe there is not another person in the house who has not paid some sort of homage to the queen of the occasion."

Geoffrey laughed. "The queen must be a little weary, I think, and my silence must be better than a gift," he said; "but, Miss Allen, I do feel a sort of fascination at present in watching your cousin; I wonder if, when your attention is drawn, you will be equally affected. Does not that chandelier hanging just over her head strike you as painfully threatening? I have watched it for some minutes now, and could almost persuade myself I see it trembling in preparation for a fall."

Rachel looked up in momentary alarm, but the light dazzled her, and she could see nothing.

The dining room was long and narrow, and lighted by fine antique bronze chandeliers, hanging by chains from the dark oak roof. The dinner that evening being large, the table had been lengthened, and Edith's place was exactly underneath one of these chandeliers, and when attention was called to it her position was, as Geoffrey said, unpleasantly suggestive of danger. Unable to get rid of the impression, yet believing it to be entirely his own fancy, he raised his eyes to the light over and over again, and at length was so convinced that this one chandelier vibrated, while all the others were steady, that he questioned the footman at that moment at his side concerning its safety. The man glanced at it, and seeing that it looked all right, and being very busy, he gave a hasty assurance that there was nothing wrong, and passed on.

"You seem very uneasy, Mr. Poland," said Rachel, lightly, thinking what a queer man he was, and that the last thing she would have expected in him was nervousness.

"I am," he answered, "but I do not feel that I have sufficient reason for disturbing the whole party. That particular chandelier may be given to shaking for all I know; for my eyes cannot so far deceive me that it can be all imaginary."

"I think you are dazzled," said Rachel, with double meaning, for she noticed that when his eyes were not directed to the lights they were fixed on Edith, and it appeared evident to her that his former indifference had been assumed. He made no answer, but for a few minutes refrained from turning his eyes towards the head of the table.

"Will the company make speeches?" he asked presently.

"Oh, no, of course not! How dreadful for Edith!"

"I thought perhaps that on an occasion like this—when a person becomes a sort of public character for a time—it might be agreeable, but of course—good God! do you hear?" His exclamation and a sudden loud crack alarmed every one, and he sprang from his chair, reached the head of the table, and throwing himself in front of Edith, pushed her aside, as with a sway and a crash the chandelier came down over the spot where she had been sitting, and struck him to the ground in its fall.

In a moment all was confusion, and no one seemed to know what had happened; but Walter Bonar, seeing that Mr. Hilton was unnerved by his darling's narrow escape, took the command, and ordered that the room should be cleared of every one whose help was not absolutely wanted.

"Let me stay," said Edith, who had recovered herself in an almost incredible manner.

"I *shall* stay!" said Laura, who was already kneeling at Geoffrey's side, as he lay pale and insensible.

"No, no, go away, both of you; we do not know what has happened!" he answered hastily.

"We will go when you *do* know; we cannot leave him like this," said Laura, firmly; and with agony in her eyes, but an unmoved face, she leaned over Geoffrey and helped to raise his head.

" There is life in him," said old Colonel
Arnold, who had been looking at him and
feeling his heart; and in a moment or two
his words proved true, for Geoffrey slowly
opened his eyes and moved his head,
although he sank back again immediately
into unconsciousness.

"Now, girls, you must go!" said Walter,
authoritatively, and they silently obeyed.

"Where will you stay, Edith?" asked
Laura, as they went out into the hall.

"I *must* go to the drawing-room. Oh,
. Laura! did you see what happened? Did
he really save my life?"

"Yes! and now he will die himself! the
only person in the world who has ever been
kind to me!"

" Laura!"

"It is quite true! but never mind that
now; let us go in together, as loving sisters
should! Wherever you are I must be near

you, they will bring the first news to you."

Fully half-an-hour passed, almost in silence, after they went into the drawing-room, before any tidings reached them. The servants came in with coffee, but they could tell nothing, except that Master, and Captain Bonar, and Colonel Arnold were with Mr. Poland in the dining-room, with the door shut, and that the doctor was sent for and expected every moment; and even while they were speaking Laura, who was standing at the window, caught the sound of wheels, but she said nothing, and sat down quietly close to the door.

Another long half-hour passed, and Walter came in. She was nearest to him, and looked up at him silently, and he was startled by the intensity of her questioning eyes.

"He will do well," he said to her quietly,

and passed on, wishing to draw attention from her.

A heavy blow on the head from the massive bronze chandelier caused the doctor so much uneasiness that he thought almost nothing of divers bruises and cuts; but although Walter also felt that there was grave cause for anxiety, he made as light of it as he could to the guests; and as those who were not staying in the house were now anxious to disperse, he stayed for a few moments to wish them good night in his father-in-law's name; and then, before hurrying back to Geoffrey, stopped to speak to Laura in her distant corner, and found that she had fainted. Richard Allen had followed him, and Walter whispered to him to stand between her and the rest of the company. "Let us get her out if we can without any one's knowing. Poor child! although she is so quiet, she has been terribly frightened," he said, feeling unusually kindly towards his disagreeable sister-in-law; and as she began to recover herself, and every one else was engaged in saying good night, they managed to get her out of the room without being noticed, and, half carrying her upstairs, gave her in charge of her maid.

"I am sure she would rather we took no notice of her being upset, Allen," he said, as they went down stairs together; but when he got home he told his wife. "And, my dear," he added, "if you can believe in the possibility of a girl's falling in love in two days in these prosaic times, you may take my word for it that that is what has happened to Laura." And Mrs. Bonar felt it was very hard that just then she could not go to Blithefield and judge for herself.

CHAPTER VII.

FIRST INFLUENCE.

THERE were several pale and anxious faces round the breakfast-table the next morning. Mr. Hilton had been too horror-struck by the danger to which his darling had been exposed to feel it possible to make even an attempt at a night's rest, and for several hours had made periodical visits to Geoffrey's door, not daring to enter, but getting a few encouraging words now and then from Mrs. Mathewson, who sat up in her nephew's room, but stole out to give the welcome tidings of quiet rest, of which she knew Mr. Hilton longed to hear; then he crept back to his own room, stopping for a few moments at Edith's door to assure himself that she was free from his own unrest, and towards daylight he had fallen asleep in his chair.

Every one had been careful to make as light as possible of the accident to Edith, and she therefore perhaps realised less than others the extent of the danger from which Geoffrey had saved her; but she had been sufficiently unnerved to dread being alone, and had asked her little sister, Erica, to sleep in her room; an arrangement which, however, she immediately regretted, for, but for the fear of disturbing her, she would gladly have stolen out, like her father, to get tidings, now and then, of the man who had been barely civil to her, and who had saved her life.

But of all the party, if any one but Richard Allen had thought of noticing it, Laura was

the one who had evidently suffered most.
First an agony of resentful shame had
possessed her at the thought that she had
betrayed her intense anxiety, to which had
succeeded an unreasoning conviction that
the truth was being concealed from her, and
that this, her only friend, would die—die
before she should ever see the face or hear
the voice again which, in two days, had
grown to be the dearest to her in the world.
Half a dozen times in the night she had
hoped to steal unseen to Geoffrey's door to
listen, and as often the light streaming
from her father's room, or the sight of him
as he went backwards and forwards, had
shown her that he was as wakeful as herself,
and that unless she chose to ask for tidings
from him she must bear her anxiety until
the morning. Conscious of the strength of
her own feelings, she failed to see how
natural and reasonable an inquiry would

have seemed to him, and how far he could have been from thinking her foolish for solicitude concerning the man who had saved her sister's life; and oppressed by the same consciousness, she would not allow herself to make inquiries from the maid who called her in the morning, into whose care Walter had given her half fainting the night before. She would bear anything rather than betray herself further, and was disgusted at the sight of her heavy eyes and white cheeks, which, if any one cared to notice them, must bring remarks. But she timed her going down with care, and met Mrs. Mathewson outside Geoffrey's door.

"Have you had a good night?" she asked, tremblingly, standing with her back to the light, and leaning against the banisters for support.

"Yes, my dear, thank you, much better than we expected, and although his head is still confused, he knows me quite well this morning," answered Mrs. Mathewson, cordially, pleased with her unusual sympathy.

" He is not—he will not die?" faltered Laura.

" Please God!—no. I do not think we need fear that. The doctor is with him now, and I have not yet heard his report; but I could see that he thought well of him at the first glance."

Again Laura felt sick and faint with the sudden relief, but this time she was mistress of herself; and just then Richard Allen came out of his room, and noticing her pale face, with a kindly joke drew her hand within his own, and kept her for a moment or two at an open window, while he congratulated Mrs. Mathewson on the success of her night's nursing.

" I believe we shall have this interesting

invalid about amongst us again in a few days," he said, " and then we other fellows will be nowhere in comparison with him ; so I give you notice, Laura, that I shall expect you to be very kind to me until he reappears to claim attention from you all."

Laura looked at him gratefully. Was the world changing all of sudden that people should begin to be so kind to her ? And somehow Richard spoke so lightly, and seemed to think anxiety so natural, that she no longer shrank from the thought that he had known of her weakness the night before.

Breakfast was half over when Mr. Hilton came hurrying in.

" I must apologise for my absence," he said, " but I am sure that all my guests will feel the claim of the injured one, and I am glad to tell you that the doctor thinks well of him. But, I am afraid we must give up the dance to-night, Edith, the music might penetrate to Poland's room and excite him, so I shall leave it to all you young people to do the best you can to make up to our expected guests for their disappointment."

"Surely you will put them off!" exclaimed Laura, hurriedly.

"No, my dear, I scarcely see reason for that; but you must put your heads together and get up a play or something for their amusement. It is not every day in the year that Edith's birthday comes, or that we have so many friends gathered round us, or——Well, Peter, out with your great idea, I see by your face you have one."

"A sort of May-Queen business would be the thing," answered Peter, gravely. "Put Edith in a high chair and crown her, and some one might write an ode and recite it."

Edith laughed merrily. "Thank you, Peter, I hardly feel up to the position."

"But we would support you, we would

see that it did not weigh too heavily, or rather "—here Peter took advantage of a general move, and stood close by his cousin —" if only you would authorise me, I would support you and return thanks in your name; I could take all day to think over the most appropriate terms."

Again Edith's laugh of amusement attracted Laura's attention, and she turned to look at her with undisguised contempt for her want of remembrance of Geoffrey, and of her own recent danger, which did not escape the notice of Captain Bonar, who had ridden over to breakfast.

" It is odd how habit has blinded all their eyes," he thought; "it never strikes them that poor little Laura can have any feelings, while to me they are plain enough. But somehow, except to Janet, I should feel it a sort of desecration to speak of them. I could never have believed that I could think so kindly of her. I wonder if that prig, Poland, knows the impression he has made."

He would have wondered still more if he had passed along the passage leading to Geoffrey's room a few hours later. Mrs. Mathewson was helping Edith to receive her guests; the servants were busy in their various places, and no one was left with the invalid but the trained nurse sent in by the doctor. Whether Geoffrey's brain was more disturbed than had been imagined, or whether the bustle of preparation and arrival had penetrated further than was anticipated, was doubtful, but scarcely had the evening's entertainment begun when he became wildly excited, and beyond his nurse's control. Over and over again she rang the bell, but in vain, it rang only into the servants' hall, and that was for the time deserted, Edith wishing every one to share in the amusement of seeing the hastily-got-up, but admirably-managed, charades which had taken the place of the intended dance.

Quiet—absolute quiet, the doctors had ordered; but how was one unfortunate woman to quiet the ravings and tossings of a strong man in delirium? How many times she had vainly gone to the door to call for help she could not have counted, when looking hopelessly along the passage she saw a lady coming towards her.

"Oh, ma'am!" she cried, "please go and send the master here, or send for the doctor! the gentleman's quite off his head, and has frightened the life out of me."

"Let me come and speak to him," said Laura. She had stolen away from the company just to pass by the door and hear that all was quiet. "Don't be frightened, nurse; we will send at once for the doctor if there is any need;" and with perfect self-command, now that there was no one to watch her

Laura went in and stood by Geoffrey's bed-side. He looked at her, but did not recognise her.

" The lights !—the lights !" he cried ; " I tell you they *do* shake above her head ! Nonsense, it is *not* the servants' steps, the others are still. Don't you see—it sways ! Oh God, it is falling !" and he would have sprung up but for Laura's detaining hand.

" Lie still," she said with authority. " Move the light away, nurse. See—there is nothing to fall. Think of the oak wood, and the blue bells, and the pheasant stretch-ing himself in the sun, and the primroses are so sweet—you said they were so sweet." She took some from a glass at the bedside, and held them to his face. He lay still for a moment or two, seeming to enjoy their fragrance. " Laura ? it was Laura went with me—not Edith !"

" Yes, it is Laura with you now, Edith is

not near," she answered, jealously. " I will stay with you if you will be quiet." He murmured a few unintelligible words, and almost before she had finished speaking his heavy eyes closed.

" You're a wonderful young lady for sure !" whispered the nurse. " You can manage him a deal better than I can !"

" Yes," answered Laura, hurriedly, " I can manage him; but I shall leave all the trouble to you, and not come again, if you say that I have been here."

" Bless you, miss ! it's not for me to talk of the young ladies of the house !" said the nurse, making a guess; and Laura, without noticing it, went on—" I must go now; but if you think it safe to leave him for a moment I can show you my door, and you can call me at any time if he wants me." And then, seeing that she could do no further good, she first sent a servant to stay

within the nurse's call, and then went back
to the drawing-room, before she had been
missed by any one but her watchful brother-
in-law.

"Just let it all alone, and make no
remarks," was the advice Captain Bonar's
wife had given him, when he had mentioned
the subject to her. "Nothing could be
better for us all than to have Laura taken
off our hands; and if she really likes him it
may make a different person of her, not to
mention the use that her ten thousand
pounds may be to him." And having a
great opinion of Janet's good sense, he
observed in silence.

The hurriedly-arranged theatricals were
received with indulgence by the guests,
who although disappointed, were determined
to make the best of everything; and if
Mr. Hilton's undisguised pride in his
daughter and heiress did bring a smile to

many faces, it was a kindly one, and all agreed that Edith was in truth a charming and gracious hostess.

Many were the conjectures as to who would be the fortunate winner of such a wife with so fair an inheritance; and not Mr. Hilton only, but others who were interested in the matter, were inclined to look with special favour on young Mr. Offord, who had just come home from India in consequence of succeeding to large property in the neighbourhood on the death of a cousin.

Bernard Offord and the Hiltons had been playmates years before, and he felt far more at home at Blithefield than at the gloomy mansion at Offord Park, which was only separated from it by a high paling. A tender little sentiment concerning Adelaide had kept the remembrance of the Hiltons fresh in his mind during his eight years' absence, and when he had heard of her marriage he had imagined himself to have received a blow, but somewhat to his disgust he found that he got over it immediately, and when for the first time this evening he met Edith grown into a woman, he felt that fate had been good to him in keeping him a free man until they met again; and her pleased greeting of the "Bernard" of old days completed the conquest, begun by her beauty and gracious manner, as he watched her attentively from the other end of the room before claiming her acquaintance.

"My dear boy, you will find that you have not lost your old place amongst us, although two of the nestlings have flown since you were here last," said Mr. Hilton, kindly.

"And the third?" asked Bernard, with hesitation.

"The third is all that a father's heart can desire, and that is saying a good deal from a man who wanted a son," answered Mr. Hilton.

But as Bernard watched Edith with attention he was not surprised at her father's estimate.

———————

CHAPTER VIII.

NEW VIEWS.

IN a few days Geoffrey was considerably better, and able to assert himself. "For Heaven's sake, if you want me to keep my senses, keep Mr. Hilton out of the room!" he said to his aunt. "He comes in here bothering about his gratitude until I am sick of his daughter's name, and he says he means to bring her to speak for herself, but that I *won't* have!"

"No, no, my dear boy! she shall not come until you are much better," answered Mrs. Mathewson, soothingly.

"Now, if it was the quiet, ugly one it would be different," Geoffrey went on; "I should like her to come in every now and then, with her quiet ways. I fancied she did come one night and put those horrible lights out of my head somehow."

"I don't think she did, but I daresay she would, if you like; but she is not very amiable, poor girl! and we can never quite answer for her."

"Well, you might ask her if she would come, but keep the heiress out of the way."

Mrs. Mathewson, fond as she was of her nephew, also extremely enjoyed the society of the other visitors, and was glad that Laura quietly, but willingly, agreed to take her turn of sitting with the invalid, and helping to while away the tedious hours.

"Ma'am, you may tell me to do my duty, and see that the gentleman don't excite himself, but it's my belief, that watch as I may—and will—the young lady knows better than either of us how to keep him quiet," said the nurse, when Mrs. Mathewson called her aside to give her instructions; and no doubt she was right, for Laura, who had brought her embroidery frame, seated herself at Geoffrey's side after a brief greeting, and appeared so absorbed in her work as to be unconscious of the restless eyes which at first followed every movement of her hands, and then gradually closed as the patient, as if soothed and satisfied, sank into a quiet sleep.

"Laura," was his first word on waking, and the ill-tempered, neglected, saddened daughter of the house could not for the moment answer him for sudden, happy tears.

"Dear child!" he said, greatly touched by her quiet care for him. "Have you been sitting here all this while?"

"It has not been long," answered Laura, quietly.

"Lor' bless you, sir, the young lady hasn't stirred hand nor foot this hower!" said the nurse, bustling up.

Geoffrey turned irritably away. "I do not want any thing," he said, ungraciously. "And you need not trouble yourself to stay while Miss Hilton is here. Are you tired of sitting there, Laura?"

"No, indeed! I like it. You have had a good sleep, cousin Geoffrey."

Although he had refused to claim such relationship with Edith a few days before, coming from Laura it pleased him, and put their intercourse on a comfortable footing.

"Do you know," he said, after watching her for a few minutes, while she went on with her embroidery, "I believe it pleases you for me to be ill, you look so much happier than you did before this wretched accident."

Laura blushed deeply, for indeed it was

true. "Of course I am happy that you are getting better," she answered hesitatingly, " and I am glad too that you like me to be with you; you know, there are not many people who care for my society."

" Poor child!—or rather it is their loss if they do not know the value of such un-obtrusive sympathy. But—tell me, Laura —did you come in one night—I am not quite clear how long ago anything hap-pened—and bring me primroses, and drive those lights out of my head?"

"Yes, you were talking so loudly as I came along the passage that you frightened me, and I came in to see what was the matter."

" I was sure you did, but that old woman who watches me like a snake would have it that it was my fancy."

" That was my doing; I told her to say nothing about it. I thought perhaps you

might not like me to have come, but indeed
I could not help it."

" I can forgive you," answered Geoffrey
smiling, and wondering to himself whether
when he got well again he should think
Laura ugly, as he had done at first, and
it was only the weakness of his invalid
condition which now made her appear
pleasing in his eyes.

" How long do you suppose the doctor
will condemn you to be my entertainer?"
he asked, after a pause.

" A week or two—I scarcely know—you
must not go too soon," she answered.

" No, I shall not wish to. Fancy being
laid up with no one, or—is it wicked?—
only the kindest of aunts to cheer one's
dreary hours! Don't flatter yourself, Laura,
that you exactly amuse me, but it is
something to know—I don't mean that
exactly, but to have a sort of idea that if

I asked you to do—what shall I say?—
catch that cock pheasant we saw the other
day, you would try to do it—just to assist
my recovery, you know."

"Of course I should," answered Laura,
simply. "But no one ever asks me to do
anything."

"Why?"

"I don't know—yes, I think I do—it is
because most likely I should refuse to
do it."

"Why?—again."

"They do nothing for me! They are
ashamed of the ugly sister. They throw
me a kindness now and then, but I do not
care to take the trouble of catching at it,
and they seldom waste their labour."

"Is that all their fault, Laura?" asked
Geoffrey, gently.

"Oh, I do not know!" she cried, hiding
her face in her hands. "Even mother did

not love me, I was always stupid or naughty, and I did not care to be anything else, and I never have cared! I never was like the rest, and no pains were wasted on me. Do you wonder if I *liked* to give trouble, and be as different as I could ?"

"I think I fully understand your feeling," answered Geoffrey, after a pause. "I—like you—have never known the real meaning of home life, but then *I* have never had the chance."

"Nor have I," said Laura, more quietly. "But all this talk of worries and difficulties is not good for you now. Give me sympathy when you are well again, but at present my work is to do anything I can to make the hours seem to pass more quickly."

"They would be very long but for you. I hate having a fuss made over me, and it is difficult to make people understand that it is worse to be bored than to be in pain."

"Is it? I am glad of that! I am so often bored, but I know little about pain and have always dreaded it."

"You look delicate."

"I am not. I have not Edith's colour, or Erica's high spirits, but I have good health."

"Then why, without the excuse of bodily weakness, have you made so much less of yourself than you ought?"

"I had no motive," began Laura.

"Oh, foolish child!" interrupted Geoffrey. "Has any one need of a stronger motive than that of making a better man or woman of themselves?"

"To what end?" asked Laura, hopelessly.

Geoffrey hesitated. "You have been brought up to believe in another world after this troubled, perplexing, yet pleasant and beautiful one?" he said presently.

"Yes, of course I have been taught that."

"Do you believe in it?"

"I don't know, I am not much fitted for it."

"There it is! you have answered yourself now!"

"I do not see what you mean."

"You say that you are not fitted for a higher life than that of this world, which in your case has been exceptionally small and poor, and yet you say you have had no motive for making more of yourself!"

"I see, but——"

"Wait a little, this question is too deep for us to enter upon it until you have thought over it; it would be like setting a child to read a Greek play before he had mastered the alphabet; but there is one

suggestion I should like to make to you—
you would get on much better with yourself
and with other people if you were more
self-satisfied."

Laura looked puzzled. "Self-satisfied?"
she repeated; "then, of course, you don't
put the same meaning to the words that
I should."

"Why not? Do you think it is wrong
to be self-satisfied?"

"I have always heard it said so."

"I daresay—but on what grounds?"

"Because—because—we all make our-
selves disagreeable and do wrong sometimes."

"Of course we do, but that is no reason
why we should not try to make an approach
to perfection, and, therefore, to self-
satisfaction, whereas it seems to me that
you have thrown the whole thing up as
a bad job."

"It seemed so hopeless, and with no one to help me!" said Laura, sadly.

"No doubt it did, but perhaps now I can help you a little," said Geoffrey, holding out his hand, and feeling immeasurably older, and wiser, and nearer perfection than his companion.

"Tell me a little more of what you mean," said Laura, feeling so happy, as he looked kindly at her and held her hand, that she no longer found difficulty in believing that even for her the heights to which Geoffrey pointed were not unattainable.

"My view is," he answered, "that some lives have been perfect, with all the perfection of which they have been capable, and those people have a right to self-satisfaction; they have used the powers they possess to the uttermost; they have made the most of their lives and gone as far as they could go; they *ought* to be self-satisfied."

"But you would rob people of high ideals of perfection."

"Not at all; but I say that a person whose. ideal is not higher than he can fulfil is likely to lead a better life, and do more good to his fellow-creatures, than a man who aims higher than he can reach and impresses himself and others with a sense of failure. In the first case a man is self-satisfied, and would lose his life rather than that satisfaction; he lives his best and highest, and a sense of self-depreciation would be ruin to him. In the second case a man may be striving his utmost at times, but he feels that it is allowed him by others and that he himself can excuse a failure now and then. He feels that he is what people would call a 'fallible creature,' he is not supported by that grand self-satisfaction which is as the breath of his life to the other, and the failure of which from my point of view is moral disease—if not death."

" This is rather beyond me," sighed Laura.

Geoffrey drew away his hand, which was touching hers, impatiently. " That is just one of the things I quarrel with you about," he said. " You take it for granted that your capacities are small, and you save yourself a lot of trouble by doing so ; but as you could not expect to get to the end of a journey by sitting down hopelessly by the roadside, so you can never improve yourself if you make up your mind that it is impossible. You are very ignorant, my dear, and therefore very helpless ; I tell you so from the height of my superior wisdom " — Laura returned his smile of amusement: " But the remarkable ingenuity and tenacity you have shown in keeping yourself in a wrong position towards the world, and especially towards your own family, for all these years, shows that at least you are not wanting in capacity and firmness."

Laura blushed deeply, and felt as if she ought to resent this plain-speaking, but could not.

"Now I have given you a good lecture," he said, holding out his hand again; "and if you are not too much offended, I should like you to think over it and tell me your conclusions some time. Now I hear my aunt's voice, and she will say I have talked too much. Are you angry, Laura?"

She clasped her other hand over his in silence, and to his surprise he saw that her eyes were full of tears, and she hurried away, not venturing to trust her voice in answer, and fearing to attract her aunt's attention.

"Like Undine, the child's soul has to be found," thought Geoffrey to himself, as he turned his head on the pillow and closed his eyes that Mrs. Mathewson and the nurse might leave him undisturbed.

————————

CHAPTER IX.

CONFIDENCES.

AT the end of a fortnight Blithefield was
nearly empty again, and Mrs. Mathewson
was impatient to get back to town as soon
as Geoffrey could be moved without risk.

Edith had made the house cheerful and
pleasant for her guests, although many
festivities which had been planned beforehand were given up, every one feeling that
they would be out of place while Geoffrey
was lying ill. It was true that the
Wedgwoods and Allens, and others not
immediately concerned, often forgot the
invalid's existence; but they all agreed
that the household party was far pleasanter

than larger gatherings, and were not disposed to find faults in any of the arrangements made for their benefit. Mary Verney, who from the first was treated almost like a daughter of the house, soon became a favourite with every one excepting Peter, whose high-flown conversation was a constant irritation to her, although at the same time she wondered that Mr. Hilton and Edith allowed Erica without rebuke to turn him into unceasing ridicule. It was no doubt most tempting, and every one seemed to think it justifiable; but she could not consider it so, nor could she bring herself to listen patiently to him, but persistently avoided him; and he, finding that she neither laughed at his "ponderous pleasantries," nor seemed interested in his long-winded stories, considered her "a most unintelligent young woman," and wondered that Richard Allen, who was

considered clever, always found so much
to say to her.

Bernard Offord had been called up to
town on business almost immediately after
his re-introduction to the Hiltons, and had
had little more than time to discover that
Blithefield had not only lost none of its old
charms, but that they were, if possible,
increased, and that the welcome he received
there was everything he could wish. In
the meantime he was looking forward to
meeting Edith in London, and was as
impatient for her arrival as Mrs. Mathewson
was to take her there; and she herself was
distressed at being unable to avoid feeling
irritated at the delay, while she was
conscious that gratitude to Geoffrey should
have made his well-being her first consideration. The unwillingness she had felt
to leave her father, when the plan was first
proposed, had gradually passed away; after

all, it was to be for such a short time, and
she was naturally anxious to get a glimpse
of the world of which as yet she knew so
little.

"I wonder very much how you and I
will get on in our change of places, Edith,"
said Mary Verney, in one of the endless
conversations which they held together
during these trying days of waiting.
"To tell you the truth, my heart fails
me a little."

"So does mine," answered Edith, laughing.

"Your comfort," Mary went on, "will
depend very much, I expect, on whether
you get on with Geoffrey Poland better
than I have been able to do; if not, judging
by my own experience, you will find Aunt
Sarah a hard taskmistress."

"Well, you see," answered Edith, slowly,
"I suppose I shall have an advantage which

you had not; Mr. Poland has so sought Laura's society that I can scarcely look upon him in any other light than as a probable brother, and I daresay you would be shocked if you knew how grateful I feel to him."

Mary laughed. "I have heard and seen enough to tell me that Laura could be spared from the family circle," she said. "But Edith, seriously, I cannot think that marriage could prosper. Geoffrey is odiously disagreeable in his present state, but I do not refuse to see that he may be an unhewn god. I believe the precious marble—with its capacity for beauty—is there, but it needs a master hand to chisel it into form, and as far as I can judge Laura's power would be weak or perverted."

Edith was silent for a few moments. "I was rather thinking of the effect of a master hand on her," she said. "I believe that, as Walter said yesterday, such a marriage would almost change her nature; and, unpleasing as I have thought Mr. Poland, and with a clog of gratitude hanging round my neck and nearly choking me, I shall try to be pleasant to him for her sake."

Mary almost imperceptibly shrugged her shoulders; she doubted the good effect of the efforts of the charming heiress to be agreeable for the sake of her unattractive sister; but although bold in expressing her opinions, she scarcely felt at liberty to suggest this difficulty.

"I have several times wished," Edith went on, "that father would let me stay at home, and send Laura to town with Aunt Sarah. It is all very well to put me off with a joke every time I speak about it, but there is no doubt that if a few weeks of London society is of so much advantage as they say, Laura stands in need of it more than I do."

Mary laughed. "No doubt she does, and perhaps her turn will come next; but, my dear, I am a year older than you are, and of course wiser, and I tell you that you will find it a great advantage to have had even a little bit of a season before you go up to town as a bride."

"Which, perhaps, won't be for the next ten years," answered Edith. "No, I am not going to be silly enough to say that I shall probably never marry—it would be too great a disappointment to father—but really I have very little to gain by it."

"Not much, certainly, except a good man's devotion; of which, perhaps, you have never yet stood in need. No, it is true you *have* nearly all that you can desire at present, but then the day will come ——"

"Be silent, prophet of ill!" interrupted

Edith, laughing. "I mean to gather my rosebuds thankfully while they last, although, of course, I know that some day they will wither; but we prize the few flowers winter gives us almost more than summer blossoms, and I am not afraid that they will be wanting even in the darkest days."

"Well! you are a very untried philosopher," answered Mary, sighing; "but you may be a true one. And now, to change the subject, I want to tell you, that if it was not for Erica I should be obliged to draw back, and say that I could not stay here while you are away."

"Why?"

"To begin with. I am desperately afraid of your father."

"Of dear old father! Why, Mary, how can you be? He is the most harmless old darling that ever existed."

"Very likely, but he frightens me. Of

course he is everything that is polite when he is aware of my existence—which is not very often, but I fancy he does not care much for any girls except his own; and yet in spite of it I am terribly afraid he will think it his duty to talk to me when you are gone."

"I don't think he will very much. He likes to have cheerful people about him, but he is often silent himself. However, you may trust Erica for talking enough if she gets any encouragement, but even she cannot chatter to unresponsive Laura. At any rate, I am only to be away two months, and when I come back again I shall try to do all sorts of things to make up to you, if you have been dull."

"I am not at all afraid of being dull here," answered Mary thoughtfully, "but it is that I don't see that I shall be much good to any one, and—oh, Edith—how I should have enjoyed going out with you! Of course, I know it couldn't be done; I couldn't afford to buy my own dresses, and Aunt Sarah couldn't give them to me, but I *do* envy you."

Edith looked at her with deep vexation. "Of course I did not know this," she said, "nor could I have done anything if I had. I don't think much about money, because I have always had plenty, but I thought you only came here because you were tired of going out."

"I will tell you the real truth, Edith. I am tired of going out when I can never afford to be really well dressed. I am tired of wondering whether this silk is too shabby or that lace too soiled to appear again. I am tired of wearing my one set of jewels night after night, but there is one thing of which I am still more tired, and which made me eager to stay here, and that is Geoffrey Poland and his cold superiority."

Edith gave a sort of shudder. "Mary," she exclaimed, "I will now tell you a real truth. I almost hate Geoffrey Poland! Remember, I have not seen him for a fortnight—not since the day he was openly rude to me, and then saved my life. Laura has talked to him day after day, but he has refused to see me, and has made me go through all this time weighted with this burden of unexpressed gratitude, and now I can scarcely persuade myself to feel grateful. And yet I must pretend to be, not only to him, but to father, who—poor foolish old darling!—thinks that a few words from me would wipe off any debt. Mr. Poland must be a hateful sort of man to let one stay in this strained position. Does he want to make me think of him incessantly? If he does, he has his wish, but my thoughts would scarcely flatter him."

Mary laughed. " I am afraid," she said,

"that I shall not flatter you when I say that I suspect he does not think very much about you—at any rate, not enough to realise that he is putting you in an uncomfortable position. He probably thinks little of what he has done for you; his nature is rugged, not small; he would despise the mean advantage of keeping up an effect upon your mind. No; I know him well enough to say that he probably feels a strong dislike to you because he has saved your life, and most likely he takes it for granted that you equally dislike him for having done it."

Edith sighed. "Oh, well, Mary, it is very evident that I ought to go to London to learn all this sort of thing. My country mind knew nothing of such feelings a few weeks ago, but it may be that at the end of my two months' training I shall understand that doing or receiving a kindness is a reason for dislike, but at present my mind is rather chaotic on that subject."

Mary laughed again. "Silly child! the whole world is not like Geoffrey Poland's perverted phases of temper, and it is of these I have been speaking, perhaps, after all, unnecessarily. His fancies were paramount with Aunt Sarah when I was there; but then, you see, proud as she is of me, I am not of much importance, but Miss Hilton is a different person altogether."

Edith interrupted. "Mary, I think Erica must go back to school again. I feel I cannot trust her with you; you are as uncharitable as Laura herself."

"I know, and I am quite half-ashamed," answered Mary penitently. "I promise you that Erica shall not know my wicked feelings; but it has been a relief to say it out to you, and besides, I feel bound to let you know that while I seem a quiet, easy-going sort of person, I feel in reality like a dormant volcano."

"We must all walk delicately, then, for fear of putting a foot through the crust," said Edith laughing. "But seriously, Mary, I do not think you will feel any necessity for an eruption while you are here. Thanks to father's guidance, I believe we lead good and pleasant lives at Blithefield; there is plenty to do, and it always seems worth doing."

Mary sighed. "Is it not something in yourselves which makes you think so? Perhaps Laura and I cannot feel quite the same."

"Laura does not, I know," answered Edith; "but then, she is not like other people—but there is father calling me and I must be off."

"No wonder she thinks her life good and sufficient," thought Mary. "I am inclined to doubt Aunt Sarah's wisdom in taking her away if she wishes to study her happiness. She won't come back the same Edith, who is perfect in her father's eyes, and I am afraid he will be just a little disappointed."

Then she stood at the window, watching the father and daughter pacing up and down the broad carriage-drive in the warm spring sunshine, deep in talk, and she grieved a little for both of them in their coming separation, short though it was to be, and wondered whether Edith when she returned would be able to give again the whole-hearted attention with which she now received every word and wish of the father who adored her.

"I don't mind telling you, darling," Mr. Hilton was saying to his daughter; "that since I have seen this strange fancy which Poland has taken to Laura, I am much happier about your going with your Aunt. She tells me that I have no business to judge of him by his decidedly unpleasing manner, and that in reality he is a sort of demi-god. It may be so, but it would have been a blow to me if *you* had discovered it."

"But you would like him for Laura, father?"

"Certainly, if she has a mind to him. I shall make no objection; *she* is not to be mistress of Blithefield."

Edith was silent for a minute or two. "Father, I wish sometimes that there was no thought of Blithefield between you and me," she said presently, putting her arm through his and leaning against him. "I do so want you to love me only for myself, and not because you fondly think me worthy of my place."

"My darling!" he answered fervently,

"if I had the best son that ever man was blessed with, you would still be first in my love. It may be that I have taught you to think too much of wealth and position, but I have not spoilt you. You have a true, kind heart; you will be a gracious mistress when the time comes. In my poor judgment, I have done well in setting a high standard before you of the duty you owe to your place in the world; and now that you are going away from me for the first time, all I ask you to remember is—that when, some day, you bring me the husband of your choice, I shall expect him to be worthy, not only of you, but of the things which I have taught you to value."

Edith listened with reverence, and silently pressed his arm; but after a while she began again in a lighter tone. "But, father, what is to happen if no one very wise or good should ever care for me ? "

" I don't think we need contemplate that, my dear."

" But it is very likely indeed to happen," persisted Edith. " You think a great deal of me, but it does not follow that any other wise man will be guilty of such folly, and then—may I marry some one who is silly, or will you give Blithefield to Laura ? "

" God forbid ! " exclaimed Mr. Hilton, energetically. " No, dear; if such a misfortune should befall us as that you should give your heart away, beyond recall, against your better judgment, why each of your sisters will be some thousands the richer, and Blithefield will be in the market."

" And your heart would be broken, poor old father ! Well, I will try to prevent such dreadful calamities; but if I do not succeed, and insist on marrying a fool, don't you think that if Laura marries Mr. Poland, he would make a very good country squire and master for the dear old place?"

"It is time you went away, my dear, to be cured of impertinence, and to find your level; you are getting beyond me. But this I tell you, that rather than see that surly fellow lording it at Blithefield, I would even disinherit *you*, if you took a fancy to him!"

"No fear of that, father. I don't deny that Mr. Poland may have many good qualities; but I do not feel inclined to interfere with Laura."

"I should like you to come back to me whole-hearted, dear daughter," Mr. Hilton went on. "You are young and have plenty of time before you. It is only because I feel myself getting an old man that I put the thought of marriage into your head at present. I feel," he added, between jest and deep earnest, "that Blithefield church-yard could scarcely hold me if my son-in-law proved unworthy."

Edith hesitated for a moment, and then answered with heightened colour; "Choose for me, father, while I *am* whole-hearted. I have unbounded confidence in your love and wisdom."

It cost Mr. Hilton an effort to keep back the name on his lips, but he had not mentioned Bernard Offord when, a few moments after, they turned at the sound of wheels to welcome Mrs. Bonar, who had driven over with her husband for the first time since the birth of the inconvenient baby.

CHAPTER X.

SISTERS.

As the time was not yet settled for Mrs. Mathewson's return to London, Mrs. Bonar had come to beg that Edith would spend a few days with her, and be present at the christening of the new baby.

"Father can better spare you now, dear, than when Laura is mistress of the house in Aunt Sarah's absence; and as Mr. Poland has not yet appeared in public, you have no duty to him to keep you at home," she said. And Edith rather unwillingly consented to go to Daisy Lodge for three or four days.

"I suppose there is no chance of my

getting even a glimpse of your hero," Janet
went on. "I confess I am all anxiety; and
as your very devoted sister, I think I might
have an excuse for asking for an interview
with her preserver."

"It is all very well for you to laugh,
Janet," answered Edith, gravely; "but I
assure you that when you see Mr. Poland
the inclination will vanish. He is the most
uncomfortable person I ever saw; and I
consider the weight of obligation to him
under which the whole family is laid is
something almost too great to realise."

"There is nothing like modesty, my dear
Edith!"

"You don't suppose I am alluding to
what he did for me—do you?—that is
absolutely nothing compared with the benefit
of his taking Laura off our hands, and
making her happy. I tell you, Janet, that
since you have been married she has been

a perfect weight upon father and me! She will scarcely ever join in anything we do, and yet always says something bitter at being left out. She has taken half the flavour out of all my pleasures for the last two or three years."

"I know it has been very bad," said Janet, sympathisingly. "But are you not a little more sure of Mr. Poland's intentions than circumstances warrant? I alluded to the subject to Aunt Sarah the day before yesterday, and she assured me, with great warmth, that there was nothing in it."

"Yes, it is very odd!" answered Edith, thoughtfully; "but she is the only person who feels any doubt. You know, I have not seen them together—for this gentle-mannered hero refuses to see me, so I can only judge from hearsay and probabilities; but father, of course, has been with them every day, and he quite expects Mr. Poland to speak to him on the subject before he leaves. Of course, Janet, you are shocked at the open way in which we speculate about it, and, indeed, I am often disgusted at myself; but Laura *is* a trial, and you know how much happier we should be without her."

"Yes, of course I know," answered Janet, gravely; " but I pity the poor child more than any of you. I think, perhaps, Edith, that having children of my own makes me more able to feel for every one, and looking back I often think we have all been hard on Laura."

"Perhaps you are right," said Edith impatiently. "I am sure I wish her the happiest life in the world, only I shall be truly thankful if she leads it away from here."

Janet sighed—she loved Edith heartily, but she was not quite as blind to her faults

as the rest of the family, and she feared that
her father's injudicious indulgence and
admiration would go far towards spoiling a
fine character. It was a trying position for
a girl to be placed in—to be the centre of
everything, with no mother to guide her,
and no wise friend to suggest the dangers
to which her father's blind confidence
exposed her. It was little that her elder
sisters could do for her —for their position
was one of delicacy—and to interfere in
family matters was almost impossible for
them. Mrs. Paget had tried it once, but her
father had not received it well. "No doubt
you would be right in most cases, my dear,"
he said, when she suggested that a little
more guidance would be an advantage to
her young sister; "but you must remember
that Edith's position is peculiar, and I wish
her to learn self-reliance as early as possible."

And Adelaide had thought with a sigh,

that with her own handsome children round her, she was not likely to forget the peculiarity of circumstances which robbed them of what she might, not unreasonably, feel was their just inheritance.

But she was a good woman, and moderately reasonable, and knew that she had chosen for herself her humbler lot in the world, and that it was her duty to make every one feel that she had chosen wisely. She knew that it was impossible that her husband should be master of Blithefield; he had determined upon his calling years ago, before he had ever seen her, and it was as a clergyman that she had loved and married him, but— might not her beautiful boy have been the heir?

What a pride she would have taken in training him to be all that his grandfather's heart could desire! and young as he was— only four his next birthday—she believed she could already see in him the seeds of a noble character, well fitted for the position which no woman, with the best capabilities and intentions, could ever rightly fill.

Perhaps the elder sisters were rather over-sensitive concerning their position towards Edith, and she would sometimes have been glad to profit by their advice; but their cautiousness had given her an idea that they were incapable of forming opinions, when it was only delicacy which had withheld their expression; and so she had learned to depend upon herself in all matters in which she did not consult her father, and often deprived herself of the real benefit of their careful and loving suggestions.

A winning graciousness of manner, shown alike to her equals and to those beneath her, concealed from people who did not know her intimately the only serious defect in her character—a want of tenderness in feeling towards those with whom she was not in sympathy. She was fond of her sisters, Laura excepted, but her father's injudicious training had taught her to consider herself as made of different stuff from the rest of the family.

Adelaide and Janet were delightful, admirable, were the best wives and mothers in the world she believed, and were deservedly popular amongst their friends and relations. "But then," she thought with unconscious pride, "they never could understand father's ways, and nothing could ever have made them capable of managing Blithefield. I can't imagine Edgar's checking Thornage's accounts, or Walter's judging of the proper felling of timber;" but she never let her thoughts lead her to directly contrast her own home rule with that of her sisters, and was not conscious of holding herself in very high estimation.

Mrs. Bonar did not succeed in seeing Geoffrey, although she sent a message to say that she should like to make his acquaintance.

Laura came down with his answer, with a flush on her cheek, and a difference in her manner which her sister could not fail to notice.

" Mr. Poland is sorry, Janet, but he has not seen any one yet but father, and begs that you will excuse him."

" Not a very agreeable gentlemen is he, Laura?" asked Janet, smiling.

" I do not find him disagreeable," answered Laura, quietly, but with a manner which checked further remark; and she went out through the open window, and gathered a handful of fragrant, richly-coloured wallflowers, before she went back to sit with Geoffrey, in the pleasant little room which had been given up to his use, and which always went by the name of the " blue study."

Janet looked after her sister regretfully. " The child *is* changed, Edith, and it grieves me that a stranger should have done more for her than we in all these years."

Edith turned away a little impatiently. " Of course she has changed—at least she looks much brighter ; but I can't say that I have yet found the benefit. I often wonder how many words she and Mr. Poland speak to each other in an hour."

" I expect you will find Mr. Poland a very different person from what you fancy him now—at any rate, from father's account, he has taken the trouble to be very kind to Laura, and I hope when we *can* get a sight of him he will think the rest of us agreeable."

Edith felt that her sister intended to show disapproval, and was glad that Mary Verney came in just then with Erica, and the conversation changed. Two days later Laura and Geoffrey stood at the window of the blue study, looking down on the party starting for Daisy Lodge, in the waggonette which Mr. Hilton was fond of driving with a pair of handsome greys. Edith was going to stay with the Bonars for a few days, and Mrs. Mathewson, Mary Verney, and Erica were to drive as far as Dorfield, where the Pagets lived, and bring back Peter Hilton, who had being staying there for a week. Two days after Edith's return she was to go up to town with her Aunt, for the doctor had pronounced that by that time Geoffrey would be fit to travel, and Mrs. Mathewson only delayed her departure in order that she might go with him. He had not yet left the house, and had begged to be excused from joining the party down stairs; but every one was inclined to believe that it was

want of inclination rather than strength
which kept him a prisoner.

Scarcely had the carriage disappeared
amongst the trees when Geoffrey turned
from the window, saying—

"I am going for a walk, Laura; will you
come and take care of me?"

"Yes, gladly," answered Laura, understanding him well enough to know that
solicitous fear for his health would at that
moment only annoy him.

"Don't think me perverse," Geoffrey
went on, "I am quite aware that I have
made myself out to be incapable of the
slightest exertion; but, to tell you the truth,
I have been pining for exercise for several
days, and it has only been the fear of having
a fuss made over my first appearance that
has kept me in."

"I can quite fancy that," answered Laura,
laughing; "and you will find that I shall

not even say that I am glad to see you out again."

" I am sure you won't, and, what is more, I don't believe you will feel it either—you have looked quite blank this last few days when I have told you how well I feel. I believe you think me much more interesting when I am ill."

"Yes, J think I do," answered Laura, slowly, and then, with a sigh, she went to put on her hat.

" I should like to get to the top of a hill," said Geoffrey, as they went out into the sunshine. " Every breath of this delicious wind puts fresh strength into me."

" I wonder if you could get as far as the ' Look-out;' you look down over the Blithefield woods, and see the road winding about below you for miles."

" Let us try ; you are strong enough to · give me an arm at need."

" Oh, yes ; and we have plenty of time ; the others will be away for two or three hours."

Geoffrey put his arm through hers, and they walked on in silence. Laura was happy, and had no wish to talk, and Geoffrey was wondering whether before they went home again he should have spoken words which he was anxious to keep back for the present, and yet which had been many times on his lips in the last day or two.

Why he should desire to have Laura for his wife was a question which he was quite unable to answer for himself, and yet in his present mood he did desire it strongly. She had neither beauty nor talent, she was ignorant and generally unamiable ; but somehow she pleased him, he was satisfied in her presence, and missed her when absent ; but yet he mistrusted his own feeling. He had begun their acquaintance from a sort of contrariety and resentment against the world and all the pleasant people in it; but very soon he had learned to take a true and sympathising interest in her unhappy position towards her own family, which had developed into strong affection since the care she had bestowed upon him during his illness. He had studied her character carefully, and believed that he could see in it great latent power, which it would be an interesting and satisfactory task to develop. He had always scoffed at the passion of love, and did not believe that he had it in him to feel it; this quiet affection and interest was sufficient, and was a higher and purer feeling altogether, but he wished it to be put to the test of absence. He had no doubt of Laura's affection for him, she showed it in every word and look

when alone with him and at her ease;
but he did not imagine that any one else
was aware of it. When her father or
Mrs. Mathewson came to sit with them in
the blue study, she was silent and unde-
monstrative, and he thought that if he
could leave Blithefield without speaking
to her of the future, no one would
comment upon it, and he had no doubt
that she would trust him, and be content
to wait his time; but he already felt
impatient for the moment when he should
feel sufficiently sure of himself to return
and ask her to be the companion of his
life. Laura, on her part, had no definite
ideas on the subject at all. She felt a
sense of possession in him which made
her jealous beforehand of every word and
look he should bestow on others; but how
it was all to end she did not know, and
did not care to imagine. He must leave

her, of course; but he would come back again, perhaps often, and she would have his visits to look forward to, and his words and kindnesses to live upon in his absence. Of course, she had heard other girls talk of their lovers, she had seen her own two sisters wooed and won; but although she had felt even fiercely envious of the love they gained, it had never seemed possible to her that anything of the kind should fall to her share. Her own family did not love her, it was not likely that any one else would, and indeed it had seemed to her that she scarcely wished it; she hugged her loneliness and unamiability and almost found pleasure in them; but when Geoffrey came it was all very different —he was like no one else, he held himself apart, as she did, and she felt drawn to him at once. Then, when first they had talked together, she had almost taken pleasure in showing him what an unloved and unloving existence she led; and he had not been repelled, but had been interested and sympathetic, and had given her comfort, even while he made her dissatisfied with her own views and ways of life. He had not said to her, as others had, that she was altogether wicked and wrong in feeling and showing such dislike to her fellow-creatures; but he had shown her that she was doing injustice to herself, and had led her to regret her position, and to seek for the reason and the remedy.

She felt no new desire to mix in the pursuits and interests of those about her, but she seldom felt tempted now to obtrude her want of sympathy and approval. She still held herself apart, but she was willing to accord to others that right to their own ways and opinions which she had hitherto, unconsciously, demanded only for herself.

" Well, Laura ! " said Geoffrey, drawing a deep breath, after a long silence, " I wonder if your thoughts have been as perplexing as mine."

" I don't think they have been perplexing, things are much more simple than people make out! One knows whether one is happy or not."

" Does one ? " Geoffrey sighed. " There is the puzzle, Laura—does one know ? "

" I know."

" Do you, child ? " he looked at her with a compassion deep and tender, which in the pleasure it gave him seemed to be like love. " Are you happy now ? "

" Yes, quite."

" And, I am happy too—with you ; but I must go away, and then shall we be happy apart ? But," he added, hurriedly, " we will not talk of that now, for I shall come back again."

"You will?—you really will?"

"Most certainly I shall; but I cannot yet tell you when it will be."

"I do not so much mind that," answered Laura, quietly, "for I am sure now that you *will* come."

By this time they had gained the top of the hill, and reached the Look-out, as the particular spot was called which commanded a wide and beautiful view of the surrounding country. Below them lay the Blithefield woods, a wide stretch of budding brown oaks, tender green beeches, with here and there a cluster of blue Scotch pines, and then away for miles ferny heathy common, which in August was like an unbroken purple sea, but was fresh and sunny now with golden gorse and shooting heather.

They sat down on a rough seat which was placed at the best point of view, and Geoffrey still kept his hand on Laura's arm.

"The world could scarcely show us anything more beautiful than such a scene on
such a day!" he said. "I am glad you do
not want to tell me the name of every hill
and church we see! It is just the wide
beautiful earth, and that is all I want to
know."

"Yes, it is enough, but I never thought it
so lovely until to-day," she answered.

Geoffrey watched her face, which was half
turned away from him, and wondered how
much she understood of her own mind.
That his presence made her happy, and that
she had given to him the affection which she
had hitherto denied to any one else, he felt
sure; but he did not think she knew it, and
he judged that it was better for her and for
himself that she should at present remain
unconscious.

At that moment he was quite sure that
some day, not very far off, he should ask

her to marry him, but not just yet. He could not come before her father and ask for her and her fortune until he had something to offer in return beyond his own small income and good intentions; he must at least have determined on some way of earning a livelihood; and although he did not believe that Mr. Hilton would make much objection to his being poor, and he himself had little scruple about accepting benefits from his wife's portion which would benefit both, he would very distinctly prefer that their positions should be more equal. So, while he could assure himself—as he believed he could—that his silence did not make Laura unhappy, he determined to leave matters as they were.

"See! the carriage is coming back, and we shall not have more than time to get in before them," said Laura presently, pointing to a black spot on a distant white line of road, which only her practised eyes could have recognised.

"Let us go back, then," answered Geoffrey, with a regretful sigh. "Will you come up here and watch me in the distance the day I go away, Laura?"

"Yes." And then, as was common with them, they fell into silence again; and when they came near the house, Laura drew a little apart; and Geoffrey, smiling and understanding her, withdrew his arm from hers, and they got in just in time to avoid the cheerful party returning from their drive.

CHAPTER XI.

THE BLUE STUDY.

" I WONDER if you will say that I have done
a very shabby thing, Laura," said Geoffrey
on the following Monday. " I know that
my Aunt has fixed on Thursday for going
back to town, and I have made an appoint-
ment to be there on Wednesday; for if I
travelled with her she would kindly fidget
over me, and treat me as an invalid, until
I should lose all patience and say something
which would offend her."

" I think it is rather shabby," answered
Laura, smiling; " but I can quite understand. Not that Aunt Sarah or any one else

has ever been anxious to make a fuss over
me."

"And a good thing for you, it has taught
you more than you are at all aware. But,
Laura, do you suppose she will really say
or care anything about it?"

"I should fancy she will, but I do not
know; and she will have Edith with her, so
it cannot matter to her very much."

"No, and that is another reason why I
would rather go first. I should wish to spare
your sister any solicitude she might feel on
my account; and when we meet in town I
shall be just like any other healthy commonplace acquaintance she may come across."

"But of course you must see her before
you leave here."

"Do you think I must? I am almost
ashamed to confess how disagreeable the
idea is to me."

"I am sure father will be offended if you

do not; he was speaking about it this morning at breakfast, and I think he meant me to tell you."

"Oh, well! no doubt it is a farce to suppose that I am unequal to the fatigues of society; but then you see society won't let me speak the truth, and say that I am not unable, but unwilling."

"No, perhaps not, but they know the state of the case pretty well—they generally call you Diogenes."

"Geoffrey laughed, but was also a little annoyed. He much disliked being the subject of a joke, and he also felt that it might, not unreasonably, be looked upon as a bit of affectation—this refusal of his to mix with other people; but after all, beyond giving some trouble to the servants, which could easily be recompensed, he could not see that it made any difference to any one.

" Oh well!" he said, after a pause; " of

course, if your father looks at it in that light, I must put aside my own inclination. I will come into the drawing-room to-morrow evening; but I shall regret our pleasant, quiet hours here, Laura."

Laura did not answer, she could not trust her voice; it seemed to her that with the ending of these hours all her happiness would pass away. Geoffrey guessed what was passing in her mind and was touched, but scarcely sorry. Her affection was precious to him, and he would make up to her hereafter for any pain he might cause her now. Silence was natural between them, and it was some time before he spoke again, and then apparently irrelevantly.

"I think," he said slowly, "that it is only right that a man should be alone until he has settled upon his path in the world. However dear to him the presence of a chosen companion may be, I think he should deny himself until then. Do you agree with me, Laura?"

"I do not know. I have not thought about it."

"Will you think?" he said, lightly touching her hand. "I should wish to know whether you agree with me in this?"

"I believe in it if you say it is right," she answered simply.

Geoffrey smiled; she was quite unconscious of her flattery. "Well, we will agree in believing it, dear."

And then Mr Hilton came in for his usual morning call, and Laura worked silently at her embroidery.

"You think you will be well enough to travel on Thursday, Poland?" said Mr. Hilton, after a few general remarks, wondering whether—as the time was so short —if Laura had been absent, Geoffrey would have had anything special to say to him.

"Yes. thank you, I think I may say that I have entirely recovered; but if it is not inconvenient to you. I want to get up to town on Wednesday."

Laura glanced at him with an almost imperceptible smile.

"It is Thursday. not Wednesday, that Mrs. Mathewson and my daughter propose going."

"Yes. I understand that; but I have an engagement for Wednesday, and my Aunt's maid is so accustomed to travelling that she is quite as good an escort as I should be."

Mr. Hilton looked puzzled: there was evidently something he did not understand, and he wished Laura would leave them alone. instead of sitting there silently behind her embroidery-frame. Then a bright thought struck him.

"Of course," he said, "if you must

leave on Wednesday it is quite convenient. I suppose you want to know the times of the trains. Laura, will you run up to my dressing-room and look for this month's Bradshaw, and if you don't find it there it is somewhere in the study."

"Oh, don't take that trouble," said Geoffrey. "I know there is a train about eleven o'clock."

"Much better to make sure! get the book if you please, Laura."

But when she had left them alone Geoffrey got up and walked to the window, and remarked on the beauty of the fresh young leaves, and the charms of the distant view, until Mr. Hilton got out of patience.

"I don't believe the fellow means to say anything to me after all!" he thought. "And I can scarcely call him to account for trifling with her feelings, when I have no proof that she has any; but he may be very sure that he will not enter this house again if he has been misleading us all."

"The park must look beautiful in autumn," said Geoffrey, wondering a little whether he would be asked to come and see it, but not caring much, for he meant to come before that with or without an invitation.

"Yes, of course the old trees look very fine," answered Mr. Hilton coldly, and then the opportunity was over, for Laura came back with Bradshaw.

"I should think you will be able to join us at dinner this evening," said Mr. Hilton, when they had looked out and discussed the times of the trains, which Laura had known to the minute days before.

"Thank you, if you will excuse me, I would rather not. I have been quiet so long that I shrink from a large party, but I will join you in the drawing-room for an hour to-morrow evening if I may. To night, Laura, we have those designs to finish for your embroidery."

"I cannot spare my daughter from the drawing-room this evening," answered Mr. Hilton, chillingly. "She must take her proper place in her sister's absence; it is not right that she should leave everything to Miss Verney, a comparative stranger."

"My proper place?" exclaimed Laura, looking up with her old defiant spirit. "It is the first time I have ever heard that I have one."

Geoffrey looked vexed, and Mr. Hilton uncomfortable. "You will learn it when you make the attempt," said her father, after a short pause, and then went away with a cool good-morning to his guest.

"Laura, don't let that spirit come over

you again, it grieves me," said Geoffrey, standing in front of her, and looking down at her gravely.

"Oh, Geoffrey, I am sorry!" she answered, looking up at him with tears in her eyes; "but it *was* hard to take away my last evening!"

"And harder still on me, for I shall be here alone."

"Oh, do let me come! I hate to be with them all, and no one will want me!"

"Whereas I shall, very badly," said Geoffrey, smiling. "But, dear child, it is not for me to say what you may do! you must obey your father's wishes."

Laura bent her head down very low, and was silent.

"Tell me what you are thinking?" said Geoffrey, presently.

"I am thinking that I owe my father but little duty, and that I do not care for his wishes!" she cried, with a burst of passion. "He has neglected and slighted me all my life, and now spoils my only pleasure! I will not do it!— not if——"

"Hush, dear!" said Geoffrey, laying his hand upon her shoulder, and feeling sorely tempted by her distress to break through his resolution of letting time try their feeling for each other. "You put me in a strait. Try to control this dislike and impatience, as I have to resist the strong desire which struggles against resolves which I believe to be right and necessary. We are companions in difficulty here; be brave, Laura, and let us conquer together!"

Laura hid her face in her hands to hide slow heavy tears which she could not repress. She believed in him entirely, in his goodness, his wisdom, and his affection for her, although even to herself she would not have called him her lover.

"Geoffrey," she said, looking up when she could command her voice, "I will do what you tell me, but not from love or respect for my father, for I feel neither, I will do it because you say it is right."

"Do it for that first, and other motives will come," he answered, puzzled by the extreme contrariety of her nature, and feeling that the task of guiding her would indeed be a difficult one; but he had no wish to draw back from it, although for a time he must seem to do so, and leave her to struggle a little way along the new road by herself.

Then a servant came to say Miss Laura was wanted, and Mrs. Mathewson, at Mr. Hilton's request, managed to keep her occupied until late in the afternoon, when, hastening to the blue study, weary and impatient, fretting against a new restraint,

Geoffrey read aloud to her page after page from books which he loved, and she was learning to prize for his sake.

She felt rested and soothed by the time the bell rang to dress for dinner, and Geoffrey putting his hand on her shoulder, said lightly,—

"Make yourself as pleasant as you can, my child, and if possible come by and bye and say good-night, and tell me how you have fared."

CHAPTER XII.

COUSIN PETER.

"Your preserver intends to appear this evening and claim his reward, Edith; I wonder what he expects or intends it to be," said Mary Verney, when Edith returned from the Bonars the next morning.

"Oh yes, Edie; Diogenes has really promised to emerge," cried Erica, excitedly. "I could scarcely sleep last night after father told us, I am so afraid of him, and yet so anxious to see him."

"Silly child!" said Edith, laughing; "you seem to look upon him as a sort of ogre, or else as a high and mighty personage whose presence will affect everybody; I can't myself see what difference it will make whether he is in the room or not, except that, of course, we must be very civil. I don't fancy he would at all appreciate a fuss."

"But he must be very odd or he would not like Laura," persisted Erica.

Edith, fresh from Janet's kindly influence, looked vexed. "You should not speak like that, Erica; it is quite likely that Mr. Poland may understand her better than we do, and that with him all that is good in her comes out."

Erica laughed. "That is Janet all over, with a little flavour of our clerical brother in addition; but oh, Edie! when a person has done you one kindness they are so often ready to do another; couldn't you ask him to set our minds at rest before he leaves to-morrow, so that we may have no doubt or anxiety about it?"

"You are a goose, Erica; and it is not to-morrow but Thursday that we are going."

"You are going on Thursday, if you like, but he leaves to-morrow, he told father yesterday."

"He apparently does not care for the society of ladies while travelling," said Mary. "When we were coming down here he went in a smoking carriage most of the way."

"He is a wise man," answered Edith. "There is nothing so disagreeable as having to talk in a train, if you do not feel inclined," but in her own mind she felt a little annoyed at this apparently persistent avoidance of her company.

Late in the afternoon Peter made an opportunity for speaking to her alone.

"Of course you are prepared," he said

solemnly, but looking at her with an expression of doubt and solicitude.

"Prepared?" questioned Edith, with surprise, she was too well accustomed to him to be alarmed. "Why, Peter, has anything dreadful happened for which I need be prepared?"

"Of course, I mean prepared with your speech to Poland when he comes into the drawing-room to-night."

"I have not the least intention of making one."

"Not make a speech to the man who saved your life?"

"No, Peter, I don't believe in speeches."

"Well! I must say, even if it vexes you, that I think you will be neglecting a solemn duty—to say nothing of the waste of an opportunity of which you might make so much—of showing your capacity for turning the occasion to the best advantage. But perhaps, Edith," and here Peter spoke low, and came near her, half drawing a paper from his pocket, "perhaps you scarcely know what to say, and I have prepared a sort of rough draft of a simple and appropriate speech which could not fail to please Poland and every one else."

Edith laughed heartily. "Thank you, Peter, I do not doubt that it is beautiful; but I scarcely think anything of the kind will please Mr. Poland; he knows that I am deeply grateful to him, and I do not think he will expect me to tell him so."

"How can you have such a poor opinion of your position and responsibilities!" exclaimed Peter, with some impatience. "But perhaps it is natural that a woman should not rightly understand these things, and if you liked to depute me to make your acknowledgments I think I can promise you that they would be made suitably, and in

language which would do you no dis-
credit."

Again Edith's merry laugh disappointed
him.

"Perhaps," he said stiffly, "you have
been beforehand with me, and have already
expressed your gratitude, but if so it would
better become you to tell me plainly than
to turn my carefully-considered—and I may
say judicious—suggestions into ridicule."

"I am not doing that exactly, Peter,
indeed I am not; and I have not even seen
him!" cried Edith, still brimming over with
barely-suppressed laughter. "But the whole
idea of my making a speech to that solemn
Mr. Poland, who no doubt intensely be-
grudges me the safety of my small brains at
the expense of his own, is something too
absurd. Of course, if there was the least
fear that his injury was more than a mere
passing one, I should be too much grieved to

have a laugh left in my whole composition, but when every one says that he has perfectly recovered, I think I may be excused for seeing that there *is* a comic side to this painful load of gratitude which I owe to a man whom I particularly dislike."

"If you dislike him and feel your gratitude a burden, it is all the more reason for expressing yourself with care and consideration, and if you will treat the matter seriously, Edith, I wish to say that it is one of peculiar interest to me, and I think that acknowledgments made at my suggestion would be particularly suitable."

"Oh, Peter! I almost believe you are going to make me an offer!" cried Edith, who found it impossible to be serious.

Peter looked highly important and complacent. "Indeed, my dear Edith, you are not far from the truth, but I was debating in my own mind whether I should speak before your departure for town—an engagement is a great safeguard to a young woman thrown for the first time into the whirlpool of society; but perhaps you have scarcely time now to think over all the advantages, and it might be better that it should not be spoken of until you return home."

"Then you feel no doubt that it will be the best arrangement for both of us?" said Edith, who felt the temptation to draw him out was too great to be resisted, and only wished that Mary was there to listen.

"No, my dear cousin, I feel no manner of doubt. Our being of the same name is no mean advantage, and then I have known you from childhood, and there are only a few minor points in which I should wish to make radical changes in your character. Your father, I know, holds me in esteem, and will not, I am sure, fail to be pleased that his—may I say rather giddy young daughter"—here he smiled indulgently, "should have a judicious guide for her inexperienced feet."

Edith could control herself no longer. "Oh, Peter!" she cried, with a laugh of such genuine and irrepressible amusement that he shrank a step or two away from her. "I don't suppose you have the least idea how utterly and entirely absurd the whole idea is to me. I can scarcely for a moment believe that you mean it as anything but a joke, and in that light it has been most successful, but it has gone far enough, and I should like you to forget it—as I shall. Now, I must run away, for father wants me."

"Indeed, Edith!—I beg,—It is nothing of the kind!" stammered Peter, and he held out his hand to detain her, but she passed him quickly, and only turned as she half opened the door.

"We will be very good friends, Peter, but I don't like your joke, and will never listen to another word of it."

Then she hastened to her father's study. Peter's offers were always common property, and she had no hesitation in speaking on the subject.

"Oh, father! that dear old Peter has just done his duty and offered to be a buffer between me and the vanities of the world," she cried, seating herself in her own particular low chair beside him.

"Poor Peter! One more bid for Blithefield! Well, my dear, have you accepted with gratitude this substantial safeguard?"

"But really, father, it was very annoying, especially as there was no one else there to enjoy the joke."

"Yes, and it is one that has been carried quite far enough. I must give him a hint. I believe he is in reality perfectly single-minded, and has no thought of being a fortune-hunter, but in our more worldly eyes it has an unpleasant appearance. But —tell me—how did it come about?"

"Oh! he wanted to write a speech for me to make to Mr. Poland to-night, and then went on to say that no one could have a better right to do it than himself."

"I see. I was afraid, my dear, that a spirit of mischief—in which you are not always wanting—might have tempted you to lead him on."

"Perhaps I did a little, father, after he had begun, but not at first. Oh, I do wish you had been there to hear him, and see his solemn manner. We always told Adelaide and Janet that when he proposed to them it must have been the most amusing moment of their lives, but they would never tell us about it."

"Of course not; and I hope you will show equal discretion."

"Oh, father, really Peter does not count! It would be so different with any one else!"

"Nevertheless, my child, I cannot have him made a laughing-stock for giddy girls, as your own good taste will show you after a moment's thought."

Edith looked very blank. "Do you mean that I must not even tell Mary and Erica?"

Her father laughed. "So that's too much to expect of you? Well; if you *must* have an outlet, I don't mind your telling Miss Verney; she seems tolerably discreet, but Erica is an irrepressible child, and she could scarcely resist ridiculing your solemn lover to his face."

"But *is* he my lover, father? I can't for a moment believe it."

"Not as we should use the word, dear; but according to his own standard he believes himself to be. He feels a good deal of honest affection for you; he has a great liking for Blithefield, and a very good opinion of himself. A combination of these feelings is too much for him, and he forgets the construction the world in general would put upon his desire to marry you, although at the moment it is sincere enough."

"I suppose he was equally sincere when he proposed to Adelaide and Janet?"

"No doubt, but they were too discreet to bring the tale of their conquest straight to me. In one case my knowledge of it was the result of my own observation, in the other of inference."

"A speech almost worthy of Peter himself, father!" said Edith, getting up and kissing him; "as you say I may tell Mary, I must go and do it at once. After all it is a great advantage to have something to take off my thoughts from the meeting with Mr. Poland."

"You are but a silly girl still, my darling!" said her father, fondly, "but you understand my wishes and ways from top to bottom, and you can be wise enough when the humour takes you."

"Yes, father, I am 'the master in petticoats,' as nurse used to say, and looking at you from that point, it is astonishing how very inferior the rest of mankind seem in comparison. But, however much you may scold me for being silly, and laughing at Peter, I am sure you are like me in this—that you would give a good deal to see that speech which he has prepared for me."

"I should have no objection, certainly; it would probably be amusing."

"Amusing? I should think it would, indeed! and father, I should not be in the least surprised if he showed it to you, he won't like it to be quite wasted, and it will be a good opportunity for you to lament together over my want of wisdom."

"Well, my dear—if I do read it it will not benefit you, for honour will oblige me to be silent about it."

"We shall see," said Edith, laughing, as she hurried away to find Mary.

CHAPTER XIII.

AN ORDEAL.

LAURA looked forward to the evening with great anxiety. Geoffrey had given her so much sympathy and such pleasant companionship in the many hours which they had spent together, and had so evidently prized her society for her own sake, that she had learned to put a new value on herself, and longed to see whether other people would do the same. She had no wish to obtrude the feeling which she and Geoffrey had for each other, but she earnestly desired that it should be seen and recognised, that every one round her should know that she, the despised and neglected one of the family, was in her turn appreciated. She could hardly have borne that her father, or sisters, or any third person should have heard those conversations in which she had revealed her sad and perverted views of life, although very often there was nothing personal in them, but she would have wished them to know that Geoffrey cared to talk to her, and listen to her thoughts on subjects beyond the small events of every day.

She did not wish to talk to him much in public, she knew that she should be almost incapable of expressing an idea while others listened, but she fervently and jealously hoped that he, too, would say little more than civility demanded. They might sit somewhat apart, but within easy distance of each other, in that pleasant silence which is only possible between friends, broken

now and then by a few sympathetic words
which would show that they had much to
say if occasion suited. She knew so little
of Edith, and of late had seen even less
than usual of her, that she had no idea
how she would behave to Geoffrey or show
her gratitude. If she was demonstrative,
he would shrink from her, but she who
was so praised for the charm of her manner
would probably know exactly how to make
her thanks pleasant to him, and then—
thought poor Laura—no doubt he would
contrast them together, and discover that
it was only because lately he had seen
no one else that he had cared to be
with her.

A few of the near neighbours were to
dine at Blithefield that evening, for Mr.
Hilton saw no reason for showing Geoffrey
the consideration of keeping the drawing-
room quiet for him, and Laura was glad

that the occasion demanded that she should
dress with unusual care, and add some of
those little adornments which until lately
she had persuaded herself that she despised. When she was ready, she went
as usual to the blue study ˙ for a few
minutes before the dinner bell rang.

"See, Laura," said Geoffrey, as she
went in, "while you were all having tea
I stole out to the gardener and made
him give me these for you," and he
held out a bunch of fragrant carnations,
shaded from crimson to the faintest blush,
for which the Blithefield hot-houses were
famous at that time of the year.

"Oh, how lovely!" cried Laura with
delight. "Somehow I never have flowers,
I have not worn them since that night—"

"When I lost my head," interrupted
Geoffrey, laughing. "No, I have noticed
that you have not. But, Laura, you must

not imagine that I shrink from the thought of that evening. I have quite got over the horror of it, and consider my recovery complete."

"Yes, I think it is, and are you very glad to get back to the world again?" she asked wistfully.

"If by the 'world' you mean the society I find in ordinary drawing-rooms, I can truthfully assure you that I am *not*, but if instead you mean man's working and fighting ground, I *am* glad, for I have to win my way there before I can venture to seek for my own personal happiness."

"But you will win it?"

"I believe I shall, at least I hope for it. Laura, you should know best how much I hope." He checked himself, for he had already said more than he intended, and it was a relief to both that almost before Laura had time to fasten the flowers into her

bronze coloured velvet dress, the dinner
bell rang.

"I suppose you can scarcely come up
here and bring me down, Laura," said
Geoffrey, smiling, as he opened the door
for her.

"I don't know; I suppose not. Do you
think I might?"

"No, dear, better not," he answered,
and sighed as he watched her down the
passage, thinking how sad it was that she,
so young, should scarcely understand the
existence of a joke. "But I will make
her happy, and teach her to laugh some
day," he resolved firmly, "although it
may be that the time will be long in
coming, and the poor lonely child may
droop and weary, and grow distrustful, but
the waiting is of necessity, not of my
choosing, and I should be a fool to kick
against it."

By way of experiment Edith had arranged
that Laura should be taken in to dinner by
a stranger, staying with his friends in the
neighbourhood. Mr. Grierson had a repu-
tation for being satirical, and abrupt in
manner, and the girls of the house in which
he was staying confided to Edith that they
found it impossible to get on with him.

" We will see what he and Laura can
make of each other," said Edith, mis-
chievously; " she has gone through a severe
course of training lately in liking the unlike-
able, and perhaps she will understand him
better than we shall." And to her surprise
she found that the experiment was successful.

Mr. Grierson was struck and also interested
by the tall pale girl with a melancholy face,
who was dressed so much more plainly than
the rest of the company, and was glad to
offer her his arm, and still more glad when

she answered his first observations in as few
words as possible, and evidently did not
expect to be talked to. He liked to be left
at liberty to enjoy his dinner and observe
other people, and noticed that his companion
took his silence as a matter of course, which
naturally after a time made him wish to talk
to her.

" You are interested in all these people ? "
he asked, abruptly, with a general wave of
his hand.

" No, not particularly. I know them all."

" What a severe speech ! Miss—a—"

" Hilton," supplied Laura.

" Oh, indeed ! I did not understand that
you were one of the daughters of the
house."

" No, probably not."

" Your eldest sister at the head of the
table has an important and brilliant future
before her, I understand ? "

"Yes, but she is not my eldest sister, there are two who are married."

"Indeed! but I understood that this one is your father's heiress."

"Yes, by a sort of family arrangement, which is a little puzzling to strangers," answered Laura, quietly.

"Your father perhaps objects to matrimony for his daughters?"

"No, not at all, but his heiress's husband must fit into his mould," said Laura, unconsciously quoting Geoffrey.

"I see, and your elder sisters' husbands did not quite fit?"

"No."

"You have another sister younger than yourself, I think,—will the property go on descending in case of continued failure, and refusal of the round man to fit into the square hole?"

"No, I believe it will go no further."

" An interesting family history, Miss
Hilton; one wishes to be intimate enough to
know it better and watch it further."

" It seems commonplace enough to us,"
answered Laura.

" Nothing can be commonplace which
has to do with your brilliant sister, I should
think," said Mr. Grierson, looking with
admiration at Edith's bright face at the
head of the table, and Laura sighed as she
thought of the contrast which strangers
must make between her and her sister, and
that she must ever expect to fade into the
shadow in her presence. It was very hard,
but as long as she could she would believe
that Geoffrey was not like other men, and
that regardless of Edith's beauty and charm
of manner, he would be faithful in his affection for her.

When the gentlemen left the dining-room
Geoffrey met them in the hall, and after

short greetings from those whom he knew, they all went into the drawing-room together. Laura was, as usual, sitting a little apart, and he went straight up to her, conscious that all who were interested in them would mark his doing so, but careless at the moment of everything but paying her an attention which he knew would please her.

After a minute Mrs. Mathewson came up to him, and with her Mary Verney, who spoke pleasantly and easily, and altogether ignored the fact that they had not met for three weeks. Then came Edith and her father, and she held out her hand and said—

"I am glad to see you again, Mr. Poland," and he said, "Thank you;" wondering whether this was to be all, and he had been fool enough to shrink from a scene which was never to be acted.

Then when Edith turned to other guests

Peter came, and fussily expressed his pleasure
at meeting again.   Half an hour had been
sufficient to restore his self-esteem and com-
posure after Edith's rejection.   She was but
a girl, he reflected, there would be plenty of
time for speaking to her when she had
sobered down a little, and doubtless after a
season of butterfly attentions she would be
more inclined to listen gratefully to his
honest proposals.   He already felt a sense
of proprietorship in her which made him
anxious to represent her in the best light to
the man to whom *he* owed a debt for saving
her life.   It would not be well that
this stranger should think lightly of her
good heart or good sense, so drawing
Geoffrey a little aside he began a studied
apology for the absence of public acknowledgments.

"We are all truly glad to welcome you
amongst us again, Poland," he said; "but

I am afraid my young cousin's somewhat giddy manner may lead you to suppose that she does not properly appreciate what you have done for her, but I assure you——"

"My dear fellow, nothing of the kind!" interrupted Geoffrey, a little rudely. "Miss Hilton has shown her good taste in ignoring an occurrence which it must be unpleasant to every one to remember;" and he turned abruptly away, leaving Peter so ruffled and disconcerted that Mary Verney, who had been watching them, kindly hurried to him, and claiming his attention, managed to prevent him from displaying his wounded feelings any further.

Geoffrey did not find the assembled company particularly interesting, and many times wished himself back again in the blue study with Laura. He spoke little to any one, and listened carelessly to music and singing of average merit, but he sat most of the time within speaking distance of her, and said a few words now and then, which made her content, without drawing general attention upon them; but Mrs. Mathewson, who had obstinately refused to believe it possible that her fastidious nephew could give a serious thought to this unattractive girl when others were at hand, watched them a little uneasily, and detecting now and then a look or smile provoked by mutual understanding or enjoyment of something that was going on, felt that her confidence in Geoffrey might after all have been misplaced, and that however much she and every one else might underrate Laura, he found pleasure in her sympathy and companionship.

Edith, fearing to seem neglectful, came after a time and began to talk to him.

"You have not been able to see much of our pretty home, Mr. Poland, but even from the windows of the blue study you can get some idea of it."

"Yes, it is looking beautiful; you will be sorry to leave it for the smoke and dust of London," he said, civilly.

"Indeed I shall, for it has seldom seemed to me more lovely than just now, and I owe it to you that I am saved to see it once more," she answered, with quiet earnestness. He bowed silently, and she turned to speak to some one else, and the dreaded scene was over. It had been well done, he thought to himself, and she had said neither too much nor too little.

"Not a very formidable business after all, Laura," he said, sitting down beside her. "Perhaps I should have paid her some unmeaning compliment. What do you think?"

"She might have expected it—I do not know;" answered Laura, slowly; "but

I myself should have preferred your silence."

"But then you understand me, and it is not given to every one to do that," said Geoffrey, laughing; and as she smiled back at him, Mrs. Mathewson, observant and uneasy, thought it was quite time to claim his attention.

When Edith sat quietly in her room that night, and thought over what had passed, she scarcely knew whether she was satisfied or not. The idea of owing one's life to another person must in most cases be painful, but when the person to whom you owe it is almost a stranger, who has yet had opportunity for treating you with marked indifference, the debt becomes indeed a burden. Prejudiced from the first against Geoffrey Poland, by Mary Verney's account of his obstinate unsociability with her, and by Mrs. Mathewson's unwise exaltation of his

character, while at the same time she confessed that his manner was often unpleasing,
Edith had scarcely had the choice of liking
him, and when added to that he had shown
no inclination to share in the kindly homage
paid to her on this occasion, as the cause
of the family gathering, and hospitality to
the neighbourhood, she could scarcely avoid
feeling irritated and offended.

She was not, however, narrow-minded
enough to forget that there were many
characters, especially amongst men, into
which she possessed no insight. Her father
she read like an open book, her brothers-in-
law were scarcely subtle enough to be
puzzling, and of other men she had had
small experience. Cousin Peter, Richard
Allen, and a few others, were often about
the house, too often for her to have thought
of especially studying them, but now she
recognised in Geoffrey something completely

new, and as it happened, disagreeable, but
certainly interesting. The most puzzling thing
about him to her was his liking for Laura,
who had persistently from childhood refused
to be one of the family, who had mocked at
offered kindness, scoffed at any attempts for
her improvement, and had been the one
daily thorn in the almost unruffled smooth-
ness of the Blithefield household. But the
fact remained, and Edith blushed that she
should feel vexed at it, he preferred un-
popular Laura to her own beloved, indulged,
and really right-meaning self. How coldly
and ungraciously he had taken her
acknowledgment this evening, and yet
she had painstakingly adapted it to what
she believed would be his liking! But
would she after all have preferred that he
should have answered it with conventional
deprecation?

"Oh, it was nothing, I assure you! of no

consequence at all, nothing to thank me
for!" No, she should have despised him
then, and with all her irritation against him
she had never yet seen reason to do that.
Well, he was interesting, there was no doubt
about it, and she a little envied Laura her
intimate acquaintance with him, but no
doubt when she saw more of him in the
prosaic light of every-day companionship
her interest would grow less, and it was
only idle for her to think much about him,
for if he was to be her sister's husband
she would probably see little of him, for she
and Laura had never been good friends, and
marriage would only still more divide them.
"But it shall not be my fault if we are
not friendly as brother and sister," she
resolved, before she went to sleep, "and I
should like somehow to prove to him that my
life *was* worth saving after all."

CHAPTER XIV.

GOOD-BYE.

WHEN Geoffrey went into the drawing-room the next morning with Mr. Hilton, to say good-bye, all the ladies of the party were there excepting Laura.

"Well, Geoffrey, it is not a long leave-taking for us, said Mrs. Mathewson, "but it would have been more convenient and sociable if you had waited until to-morrow."

"I have an engagement for this evening," he answered, shortly.

"Yes, but I daresay it could have been put off, but however that may be, you will be at home to dinner to-morrow, of course?"

"I hope so. And now, I suppose, my time is up."

"Where is Laura?" asked Mr. Hilton. "She will not like you to go without saying good-bye."

"I have just seen her," answered Geoffrey; and then, when they had passed through the hall, and he stood on the doorstep, he added, "Good-bye, sir, and many thanks for all your kindness and care."

"Oh, there is nothing to be said about that, or I must speak again of the debt I owe to you; but we shall be seeing you here again very soon, of course."

Mr. Hilton felt that this was a needful bit of fatherly wisdom for Laura, and that it was quite necessary that the young man should be reminded that attentions such as his were expected to lead to something.

"I hope so, indeed," answered Geoffrey,

earnestly; "but I have to put my shoulder
to the wheel and make some progress before
I can think of taking another holiday, even
to visit beautiful Blithefield." Then with
another shake of the hand he was driven
away.

Mr. Hilton turned back into the house in
some distress. Had he done rightly by his
motherless girl in letting this young man go
away without finding out whether he was
in earnest in his liking for her, or had
only been whiling away idle time? But
what could he have done? he could not
force his daughter upon any man, he could
not lay himself open to the charge of
wanting to get rid of her, either for her
sake or for his own, and he was even
deprived of Mrs. Mathewson's help in this
perplexity, for she refused to see that there
was reason for supposing that Geoffrey *had*
any intentions, and, although her own mind

misgave her, declared that she believed that neither he nor Laura had any feeling but friendship for each other.

Meanwhile, as he drove through the park, Geoffrey's mind was equally disturbed. Until Mr. Hilton made his parting speech, which he had done with some emphasis, he had believed that no one but himself and Laura had any suspicion of their attachment to each other—indeed, he himself had scarcely known the strength of his own feeling until Laura, white, trembling, but tearless, stood up to wish him good-bye in the blue study, with one hand grasping the table for support. He looked down into her sad eyes for a moment, and then put his arm round her shoulders.

"Laura, my love!" he exclaimed, but even then checked further words, and kissing her gravely and earnestly let her go. "I will come back, God knows, the first possible moment!" he said. "You will not be unhappy?"

"Oh no, Geoffrey," she answered, her eyes gentle and full of tears now, and at that moment she seemed to him almost beautiful; but he believed he was right in leaving her thus, and with a clasp of the hand he turned away. "You will watch for me, Laura?" he said from the doorway. She answered with a silent gesture, and he was gone.

All this passed through his mind again as he drove on, at one moment regretting his caution, and at another assuring himself that he had done the only thing that was right.

"Stop here for a moment, please," he said to the groom, as they came to a sharp turn in the road; from whence, looking back, there was a wide view of the Blithefield woods, then he stood up and waved his hat several times, and sat down again with a smile. "You can go on now," he said, and the groom wondered, and thought the "young gentleman still seemed rather queer in his head like."

One thought filled Geoffrey's mind all through the journey up to town. "I love her to-day: shall I love her in remembrance a month hence?" he asked himself over and over again, and no previous knowledge of his own character enabled him to answer the question. He distrusted himself to an extent which was painful and humiliating, and was, perhaps, unjust to her. He had felt assured years ago, when the subject had first interested him from a safe distance, that he had strength of character enough to defend himself from the ordinary weakness of mankind, and that excepting with his own consent, he would never fall a victim to the undesirable passion of

love.   He would, probably, marry some
day, rather late in life, but it would be a
woman whom his taste and reason approved
as a companion, and whose society would
embellish—but in no way disturb—his
course of life.   And yet, now he believed
he *was* in love, in love like any common
unreasoning fool!   In love with a woman
who was neither beautiful, nor educated,
nor talented, to furnish him with an
excuse, who was passed over by all who
knew her best, and yet who, first in his
suffering and weakness, and afterwards in
the long hours of returning health and
necessary idleness, had been to him the
only truly sympathetic companion he had
ever known.

"After all," he thought, "what an
absurd value each individual puts upon
himself!   I struggle and doubt, because I
am not sure that this girl is the best wife

that Providence can send me, quite as much as from hesitation over the good I can bring to her. I know that countless better men than I am go through life without ever finding what people call, 'a kindred soul;' and women without number —fairer and wiser than my little Laura— live and die unmarried; and yet I hesitate for myself and for her, and am unwilling to speak the words which would bind us for life together."

But argue with himself as he would, he still believed that it was the best wisdom for them both that they should remain apart for awhile.

CHAPTER XV.

LOST.

The party gathered round the luncheon table a few hours after Geoffrey's departure was a very small one.

- Peter—not feeling quite happy, and having an uneasy apprehension that every one in the house knew of his rejection—which yet he assured himself was only due to girlish caprice and indecision, had made the most of an indefinite invitation from the Bonars, and had gone to inflict himself upon them for a day or two before returning to his bachelor lodgings at Brighton; and Erica was spending the day with a friend at

Mornington, where her father had gone on business as a magistrate.

"Where is Laura?" asked Mrs. Mathewson, as she and Edith and Mary sat down to the table.

"I don't know," answered Edith carelessly. "She is often late. Stephens, does Miss Laura know it is luncheon time?"

"I struck the gong, miss, as usual," answered Stephens; "but I believe Miss Laura has not come home."

"Oh, it is all right, Aunt Sarah; we never wait for her if she has gone out," said Edith; but she felt a little sad for her sister, knowing that she must feel the loss of her companion and friend. But there was a good deal to be arranged and thought about before she left home the next day, and it was not until her father came home late, and said,

"Well, what has Laura been doing with

herself?" that she remembered that she had
not seen her since breakfast time. She
ran hastily upstairs and looked for her,
first in her own room and then in the blue
study, but she found her in neither.

"Miss Laura went out a few minutes
before Mr. Poland left," said Ellis, the
girl's maid, in answer to inquiries.

"And you have not seen her since?"
asked Edith.

"No, miss. She has not been in, I'm
sure, or I should have seen her thick boots
and ulster. I never knew Miss Laura do
this sort of thing before, Miss Edith."

"No, Ellis; but she must have promised
to go somewhere, and then forgotten to
tell us," answered Edith, but she began
to feel really uneasy.

It was past six o'clock now, and Laura
must have gone out before eleven. It was
true that now and then she did not come

in to luncheon, but on those occasions she had invariably come in to afternoon tea with a good appetite, and had given some sort of account of her absence. It was so unlike her to draw attention to herself in this manner, especially when there might be something to observe, and no doubt she was feeling deeply the loss of her companion —her lover—Edith said to herself, although she would not have let it pass her lips, and there was nothing to be done but just let her father know the state of the case, and leave him to judge whether there was really cause for uneasiness.

Mr. Hilton, feeling considerable doubt of his own wisdom in the management of this uncongenial daughter, spoke to Edith somewhat severely.

"You do not mean to say that you have let all these hours go by, and when your sister has not come in to luncheon or tea, have passed it over without inquiry?" he said.

"Well, you see, father dear, Laura hates being fussed over, and we all knew that she would feel dull to-day and would wish to be alone; and yet that is not quite *all* the truth, for I have been so busy that, excepting at meal times, I confess that I have not thought of her."

"You are quite sure that the servants know nothing of her?"

"Yes, father, I asked Ellis, and she said that Laura put on her ulster and thick boots, and went out just before Geoffrey Poland left."

Mr. Hilton took a turn up and down the room, and before he spoke again Mrs. Mathewson knocked at the door and came in.

"Well, have you found her, Edith?" she asked, somewhat anxiously.

" No," answered Edith, dejectedly.

" Sarah! it is not possible that that nephew of yours has persuaded the poor child to go off with him ? " said Mr. Hilton, stopping in front of her, and speaking with great agitation.

" Wedgwood! How *can* you think of such a thing ? Of course not! If you don't know your own daughter better than that, I can answer for Geoffrey."

" But you see," said Mr. Hilton anxiously, " your nephew is not quite like other people, and my poor child is different too. They have not told us their thoughts all this while, and it might be that they have taken into their heads to go off and get married without a word to any one."

" I am quite sure that Geoffrey is incapable of such a dishonourable action," answered Mrs. Mathewson, angrily.

"But, my dear Sarah, it might not be altogether a dishonourable intention; no doubt he has seen how deficient we have been in sympathy towards this poor child, and he might think that he was doing well for her; but after all it is mere nonsense to talk like this, and she may come in at any moment; at any rate, I will go and have a look for her."

Mr. Hilton went round to the stables, and in as casual a way as possible, sought out the groom who had driven Geoffrey to the station.

"You were in good time for the train this morning, Morris?" he asked.

"Yes, sir; we had a few minutes to spare."

"Ah! you were not hindered on the road then—you met no acquaintance?"

"No, sir; we never stopped at all, except just a moment when the gentleman made me pull up a-bit while he looked back and waved his hat."

"Oh, I see, to say good-bye, in case we were watching him."

"Yes, sir, I s'pose so;" and then Morris, having nothing more to say, went on with his work.

"She cannot have gone with him," Mr. Hilton thought to himself, as he went back to the house. "They certainly did not meet on the way if Morris has told me the truth, and she had not time to get to the station. The child always was odd, and has been left to take her own way, and perhaps it is only foolish to worry over her; but I will do her the justice to say that it is the first time she has caused me real anxiety in all her life."

When the dinner-bell rang at seven o'clock, Laura was still absent, and after a hurried and almost silent meal, Mr.

Hilton felt that, in spite of his dislike to calling attention to her strange behaviour, it was quite necessary that some steps should be taken to discover where she was.

"Do you think she can have gone to Adelaide, or Janet?" he asked of Edith, meeting her in the hall, as, pale and anxious, she came back from another fruitless visit to Laura's room.

"It is possible, father; we might send and inquire," she said; but she did not herself believe it would be of any use.

"Surely, Wedgwood, you cannot still think it possible that Geoffrey has taken the child away?" said Mrs. Mathewson, resentfully but anxiously, when he came back from sending two men on horseback to the houses of his married daughters.

"No, Sarah, I do not say that I think so, but I still consider it possible. In the meantime, I am going with Stephens and Morris all through the park; there is no knowing what accident may have befallen her."

"Let me come, too, father?" asked Edith.

"No, darling, it would be better not. I should wish you to be here if she comes home. God grant that it may be all a false alarm; but, at any rate, it has taught me how dear the child with all her faults is to me, and I trust to you to be kind to her if she does come."

Edith's eyes filled with tears. "I am afraid I have not been kind, father; but I feel now as you do."

It was past ten o'clock when the men returned with notes of distress and anxiety from Adelaide and Janet. Neither of them had seen anything of their sister, and it was only the superior wisdom of

their husbands, who represented that they
could be of no use, which prevented them
both from hurrying to Blithefield, but their
father might count upon their being there
early next morning.

Edith opened and read the notes, but it
was much later before her father returned.

"We have been all round the park,
through the greater part of the woods and
up to the Look-out, but can find no trace
of her," he said. "I fancied once that I
heard a faint call in answer to our shouts,
but it must have been fancy, for we could
not hear a sound again. Both lodge-keepers
say that they have seen nothing of
her, and Morris, after seeing the police,
came back by the station, but she had
not been seen there."

"Father, what do you think?" asked
Edith, putting her arm round his neck.

"I can think nothing," he answered.

"I can only feel that I have never been a father to her," and Edith could not answer better than by silent kisses.

Lights were kept burning in Laura's window all the night, and the early morning found the whole household astir again; but still there was no trace of the missing girl. Morris and another groom started off at daybreak to make fresh inquiries in every likely part of the neighbourhood, and after a hasty breakfast, which Edith came down to give to him, Mr. Hilton went out to direct the searches of half-a-dozen men who were bidden to leave not a yard of the estate unexplored.

CHAPTER XVI.

LAURA'S VIGIL.

THE point in Blithefield Park which was called the Look-out was about a mile away from the house, and was approached by a steep winding path, which although seldom used was always kept in good order. A group of enormous old Scotch firs marked the spot for miles round; and although Mr. Hilton was not too gracious in allowing his neighbours to enjoy the beauty of his estate, it was a recognised custom that during the summer months those who chose to apply at the lodge gates were allowed to visit this beautiful point of view, and admire at their leisure the huge red trunks and spreading limbs of these old noblemen of the woods.

For some yards on each side of them the ground was cleared of undergrowth, and a wide space of rough grass, broken here and there by a patch of heather and bracken, sloped down to a steep and broken bank, beneath which the oak woods began.

On one side of this cleared space a very narrow path led further into the woods, a path so little used as to be almost forgotten, excepting by any one who happened to remember that there was a point, not easily gained however, from which the winding road to the station could be seen for a greater distance than even from the higher ground of the Look-out.

It was not until nearly midday that Mr. Hilton, sick at heart of the fruitless search for his daughter, for the second time climbed wearily up the wider path to see if there were any signs of his returning messengers. He was no longer either young or active, and it was seldom now that he exerted himself to walk so far, and the fact that there was a path leading further into the woods had for the time escaped his memory; but as he stood alone under the solemn stately trees, straining every nerve to catch a sight or sound, once more he fancied that he heard the faint cry, which, after vain search the night before, he had unwillingly persuaded himself was only the result of his own anxiety. But now, as he stood there in the still morning sunshine, a shiver ran through him, as very faintly—not once—but twice at least, he believed he heard a call, "Father! Father!"

"Laura! I am here! I am coming!"

he shouted, as with a sudden recollection of the old path, now nearly overgrown, he plunged through a wilderness of withered ferns and springing heather, calling at every moment, "Laura! Laura!" But suddenly he stopped in dismay, for his way was barred by fallen bushes and mounds of earth, and looking up he saw above him a freshly-broken bank torn asunder by the roots of falling trees. "Laura! Laura!" he cried again, and then faint but unmistakeable came the answer, "Father, I am here."

He was not accustomed to exertion, and although excitement gave him strength it was several minutes before, guided by her feeble voice, he found himself beside her, where she lay half-hidden beneath the boughs.

"My child! Thank God, I have found you! Are you terribly hurt?"

"No, father, I am not hurt, I think; but I cannot move, and I have been here, oh, so long! since yesterday."

"Are you in any pain?" he asked, stooping to her, and almost fearing to hear that she had gone beyond that.

"No, I believe it is true that I am not hurt, but I am fixed down and cannot stir, and oh! I am so tired and cold!"

Her father, by leaning over, could reach her face where she lay, and he bent down and kissed her.

"You must wait a little while more, my child, while I go for help. I shall only hurt you if I try with my own strength. To think that I should have been such a thoughtless fool as to bring neither food nor wine! But God keep you until I get back again."

But even while he was speaking her eyes closed, and her white face grew whiter as she fainted away.

Hurrying back, shouting as he went, Mr. Hilton met Morris at the Look-out. A few words explained the matter sufficiently, and the groom hastened away—first to send two or three men to help his master, and then on to the house to tell Edith what had happened, and to bring back food and wine.

Mrs. Mathewson had telegraphed to her housekeeper the first thing in the morning, to say that her return was unavoidably delayed; and although she did not for a moment share in Mr. Hilton's distrust of Geoffrey, she thought it only fair to him to ask for a return telegram to say whether he had arrived.

It was, of course, impossible that Edith should leave home under the present circumstances; and when Morris hurried into the hall, too eager to go round the back way, or stand on ceremony, she was dividing her attention between a telegram

which Mrs. Mathewson had just received
from Geoffrey in answer to her own, and
anxious inquiries from Mrs. Paget, who
had driven over with her nurse and baby,
to stay with her father if he required her.

"She's found, miss!" cried Morris, breath-
lessly. "And she ain't much hurt, but just
half-starved; and Master says will you give
me food and wine to take back, and send
for the doctor."

Edith rang the bell and gave her orders
to a servant who appeared on the instant,
before asking a single question; but it
needed only a few words to explain that
Laura had been lying there helpless for
the last twenty-four hours while they had
sought her and feared for her in the wrong
directions.

Morris, starting at a run with the needed
restoratives, was out of sight before Edith
and Erica could get ready to start, leaving

orders that the low pony carriage should
follow them as quickly as possible; and while
Mrs. Paget stood at the door watching them,
Mrs. Mathewson turned to Mary, who was
close beside her, and almost whispered—

"Did you think she had gone with
Geoffrey, Mary? Do you believe what they
say is true—that he cares for her?"

"Yes, Aunt Sarah, I do believe it, and I
did think she had gone with him, but I ask
pardon from them both; and oh! how she
must have suffered! Of course, she went
there to watch for him, and has been there
all this while. My heart aches for her."

Mrs. Mathewson had known Laura and
her unpleasant temper too long to share
in Mary's extreme sympathy; but she
was obliged to acknowledge to herself that
she had been altogether wrong in the
view she had taken of late of Laura's
character.

She had believed her to be incapable of
the ordinary feelings and weaknesses with
which she had had to deal in other girls,
and now she found herself brought face to
face with what was apparently a romantic
passion, with which she could not in any
way sympathise. She had been most
foolish and short-sighted—she saw it now
—in allowing Geoffrey and Laura to be so
much together, but it was too late to
repent, the mischief was done, and she
could only console herself by thinking that
the nephew—who was as dear to her as a
son, would be doing well for himself from
a worldly point of view, if his infatuation
should prove lasting.

Laura, with her ten thousand pounds,
was not a wife to be despised, and he
seemed, to other people at least, to have a
genuine liking for her; but his aunt had
hoped that he would marry some one very

different, and had been prepared to ensure that no money difficulties should stand in his way, if he chose a wife whom she should consider worthy of him. She had had a dream—short-lived, indeed, but pleasant—that Mr. Hilton might so value Geoffrey's character, that he would be willing to overlook all shortcomings, and recommend him to Edith's notice, in such a manner, as to ensure her consent to a marriage in which one would possess wealth indeed, but the other those qualities of mind which were infinitely above sordid advantages, when it so happened that they were not combined. But she had soon awakened from such dreams. Mr. Hilton —in all unconsciousness—had made her thoroughly aware that his son-in-law, the husband of his heiress, must be heart and soul a country gentleman, and she could not but acknowledge that for such a

position Geoffrey was probably, of all men,
the most unfitted. But yet the dream was
dear, and even while softened towards
Laura, she could not feel it possible to
welcome her in Edith's place.

The return home from the scene of
the accident was accomplished quickly and
easily; but even when Laura was rested and
restored, and able to talk, it was not quite
easy to understand what had happened,
nor was she herself clear about it.

" I put my arm round a branch and
leaned forward," she said, " and then the
ground gave way under my feet, and I
fell, a long way down, and before I could
move the tree fell over me and held me
there;" and then Adelaide, who was
sitting beside her, saw that she could as
yet scarcely bear the thought of it, and
she asked no more.

" I suppose we must put off our going

indefinitely," said Mrs. Mathewson, grudg-
ingly, when she was talking to the doctor,
who, while he assured them that there
was no positive injury, said that he could
not yet foretell the effects of the long
exposure and nervous strain.

"If you will forgive my speaking
plainly," he answered, "I will say that
for Miss Laura's sake the sooner you go
the better. She is painfully anxious that
no fuss should be made over her, and I
imagine that she has some special reason—
may I conjecture that it is to save some one
from anxiety?—for making as light of the
whole matter as possible. Unless something unforeseen arises, I shall be inclined
to fall in with her wishes, and let her get
up and sit in her favourite study to-morrow.
She and I have met there many times in
the last few weeks."

He paused significantly, but Mrs.

Mathewson did not choose to understand him.

"Of course, in that case there is no reason for delaying our going," she said; "and as Mrs. Paget will be here for a few days, we may leave without anxiety."

"Oh, yes," answered the doctor, who rather disliked Mrs. Mathewson and her pronounced medical theories, and during Geoffrey's illness had learned to be interested in the disagreeable member of the family, who had done so much towards his patient's cure.

So it was settled, that as Mrs. Mathewson had many engagements in town, she and Edith should leave Blithefield the next morning, and that Mrs. Paget should stay for a few days until the household had recovered its usual calm.

That she should be left alone, safe, and warm, and quiet, with the firelight shining upon her as she lay in bed, and a soft air from the open window moving the curtains, was Laura's one desire. She was tired, and aching in every limb, and intensely wakeful, but she had no wish to sleep; she wanted just to go over in her own mind all that had happened, and come to a clear understanding with herself how far she had betrayed her desire to catch the last passing glimpse of her departing friend. There was a careful and intentional reticence in her thoughts which prevented her from naming him even to herself as her lover, excepting in moments when the thought leaped up unawares, and even then, mingled with happiness, came distrust of her own power to retain him.

She believed in him completely, he would at least be a faithful friend to her, and although he had seemed to say that it might be long before they met again, she was rich in remembrance, and could afford to wait.

She was patient and tractable, and did everything she was told for the rest of the day; she was so anxious to be well, and to have no fuss made over her, and still more anxious that Mrs. Mathewson and Edith should not delay their going, and so make the accident, which she knew *must* come to Geoffrey's ears, appear of importance.

She smiled to herself as she thought that if *she* could tell him about it she should not mind—she could make it seem natural, and he would quite understand, and be interested; but the impression he would get from the story as told by others might be very different; and yet she could not bring herself to ask them to make light of it.

When she woke the next morning she felt tired and weak, but there was no sign of illness about her, and when the doctor came he assured them all that there was no cause for anxiety, and that he feared no worse consequences than the exhaustion which might be expected from the long fasting and exposure.

Laura had been conscious that Adelaide and Edith had come into her room several times in the night, and had given her food or wine, although she had been too weary to speak or notice them much; but it made her heart soften towards Edith when she came to wish her good-bye, and they parted with affection, and yet Laura was well aware that such emotion is but passing, and leaves little mark on life.

CHAPTER XVII.

THE FIRST LETTER.

A FEW mornings after Mrs. Mathewson and
Edith left, Mr. Hilton found amongst his
letters a short note from Geoffrey Poland,
saying that he was busily trying to find
some permanent occupation, and thought
he had a fair chance of success, but for
the rest full of civil nothings, through
which ran a vein of cynicism undetected
by the receiver; but there was a postscript
which said simply—" Will you be kind
enough to give the inclosed letter to your
daughter, Laura."

Mr. Hilton was considerably perplexed.
Should he be right in allowing a corre-

spondence between these two, when Poland
had given him no assurance that he had
any meaning in his attentions? And yet
it would be hard on both of them if he
put difficulties in their way, when in his
own mind he would thoroughly approve
of their marriage. His heart was softened
towards Laura in these days—since he had
so nearly lost her—and ten to one, he
thought to himself, she knew much better
how to manage her own affairs than he
did.

So after a short hesitation he quietly
handed to her both Geoffrey's note and
the enclosure, saying—

"Poland seems busy just now, and setting
to work in earnest. I suppose we shall
not see him here again at present."

"No, father, I suppose not," answered
Laura, quietly, and went on pouring out
tea.

"O, father, do let me see Mr. Poland's letter!" cried Erica. "I always feel so curious about people's writing."

"Certainly, dear, when Laura has read it, and Miss Verney too may be interested," and Laura hurried through the note to her father, and passed it on without remark.

Geoffrey had not said a word about writing to her, and she had scarcely thought of it; but now, lying close to her hand was a thick letter, sent to her openly, and given by her father without reproof, and her happy days were not yet all over when this was allowed. It was an event for her to have a letter at all; she had no friends, and the family connections always wrote to Edith or Erica, excepting at Christmas or on her birthday, when they did not like to leave her out She could not read it in public, for then she would be obliged to speak of it, and although she had no thought of there being anything special in it, she knew that it would be meant for no eyes but her own, and that no one else could understand its meaning.

It was a recognised thing now that the blue study should be given up entirely to her use, and there she spent the greater part of every day. She knew that Mary had been asked to Blithefield especially to be a companion to Erica, and to make the house pleasanter for her father, so she had no scruple about disposing of her time as she pleased. She took away her letter to enjoy it in solitude, sitting by the open window, in the chair she had always used when Geoffrey was there. It was no love-letter, but it satisfied her fully; it was tender and sympathetic, it abounded in allusions to their talks together, it hinted at a future of less interrupted intercourse, and it seemed to her just the perfection of what she most desired.

At the end he said, "I hear that some accident or something uncomfortable happened to you the day I left, which delayed your sister's leaving home; but neither she nor my aunt have vouchsafed an explanation, and if not disagreeable to you, I should like you to write and tell me exactly what occurred."

Laura was surprised that he should have heard so little, but then she knew nothing of a conversation which had passed between her aunt and Edith as they journeyed up to town.

"My dear," said Mrs. Mathewson, "the less you say to Geoffrey about this foolish business of Laura's the better."

"Why, Aunt Sarah?" asked Edith, who did not at all approve of the light in which her aunt regarded the matter, and fully intended to be a good sister if occasion arose.

"Surely your own sense of propriety should tell you, Edith, that her rushing off like that at the risk of her neck was not becoming to any girl; and although Geoffrey might for the moment feel flattered at her wishing to catch the last glimpse of him, it would scarcely raise her in his estimation."

Edith, to whom this view had not occurred before, thought it might be as well to say little about it, especially as she really knew nothing of Mr. Poland's character, and so answered his somewhat anxious inquiries indifferently.

Laura, in her own mind, shrank from the idea which Geoffrey might get from her aunt or sister of what had occurred, but there was nothing unpleasant in telling him herself; they had agreed together that she should watch for him, and she had seen him

stop and wave his hat before she left the
Look-out. She would like to give him an
idea of what had passed through her mind
as she lay there alone and helpless all
through the long day and night; of her
strange feelings and the new knowledge
that had come to her of external things; how
the pheasants had crowed within a yard of
her head, how the rabbits had more than
once brushed by her hand, and an owl had
skimmed closely over her, and small, rustling,
unseen creatures had been moving all the
night through, excepting in the quiet hour
before the dawn, when all the world but she
seemed sunk in sleep. Even in the midst
of cold and weary discomfort she had sometimes for a moment felt glad of her new
experience, and now that it was all over she
would not for the world have been without
it. She had not been frightened; from a
child she had no nervous fear of danger or

death, life had never been so sweet that she
should greatly regret to lose it, and although
these last few weeks had taught her that
even she might be as happy as the rest, she
had not in those lonely hours greatly cared
to live. She must feel sad and desolate
until Geoffrey came back again, and then—
but she had been resolute in letting her
thoughts go no further.

Late in the morning, while she still sat
at the window with the letter in her lap, her
father came to her.

"I want to have a word or two with you,
my dear," he said, "and I came here because
I thought we should the more easily understand each other."

"Yes, father," answered Laura quietly.

"I wish you to tell me, as a guide to my
future conduct towards him, whether Mr.
Poland has spoken of any engagement
between you." Mr. Hilton had so little

experience, and still less knowledge, of his daughter's character that he did not know how to put it less abruptly.

"No, father."

"Has he made you understand that he means to speak of it at a convenient time?"

Laura's eyes dilated, and her hands clasped each other, but she again answered quietly—

"He has not said so."

Mr. Hilton began to be impatient. "My dear, I request that you answer me a little more fully. This young man has sought your society so persistently that I could not but expect that he would speak to me on the subject before he left the house, but instead of doing so he only expressed a vague hope of coming again. I wish you to understand that I told him that I should *expect* to see him, but gave no definite invitation, for I have your welfare to consider, and if he has been trifling with you it is better that you should let me know it."

" He has not."

" You understand him, then ? "

" Yes—I don't know—oh, why do you ask me, father?" cried Laura in great distress, in which, however, there was not a shadow of distrust of Geoffrey, although of course her father could not comprehend it.

" I believe I am speaking for your good," he said, " when I tell you that he will not enter this house again unless I understand the meaning of his coming, nor shall I allow letters to pass between you. I do not ask to see this one, but it must be the last, and I shall myself write and tell him that I cannot allow any correspondence. My dear, we have not been a good father and daughter to each other, but I learned that day when you were missing that you were more to me than I knew before, and I should be glad that you should come to me in trouble."

Laura who had quickly recovered herself, smiled with infinite superiority. " I am not in any trouble, father, at least not in the sense you mean. You think I am grieving over Mr. Poland, and that he has disappointed me, but you are quite mistaken. I do grieve over losing his society, for I have no companion now, but for nothing else, for I believe him to be the true gentleman he has always shown himself to me."

Mr. Hilton felt awkward, and as if his well-meant, but rather forced sympathy had been thrown back upon him. " You mean " ——he began; but Laura interrupted him.

"I don't think, father, there is any need for you to ask me what I mean. I am satisfied with his conduct, and I cannot answer any questions about him."

"You forget that you are speaking to your father, Laura!"

She was silent for a moment or two, and then answered: "It is not that I forget, but that I hardly know how I ought to behave to you as my father, for I have seen so little of you. I could almost reckon on my fingers the times that you have spoken to me in the last year until Geoffrey came, and then it was to him more than to you that I owed the few words you spoke to me each day before him."

"Laura!"

"Yes, father, I am afraid you think it wicked that I should speak like this, but remember what a hard life I have had! It is bitter to a child to be always called naughty; if you had thought about it you would have known that it could not be true, that there must have been faults as great as mine."

Her voice failed her at the remembrance of the years of blame and neglect, which yet she knew were in a great measure owing to her own perverse antagonism.

Her father took a few turns up and down the room in perplexity, and Laura, who hated a scene, and to whom a reconciliation was worse than a quarrel, strained her thoughts for an excuse for leaving him. Geoffrey would have told her to speak a gentle word, she knew, but she would rather have been shut up in her room in disgrace, as in her childhood, than patch up a hollow peace.

"It is kind of you to say that you wish to help me, father," she said at last, standing at some distance from him, and speaking slowly; "but you see I am in no want of help, and not being accustomed to kindness, I scarcely know how to take it."

She meant her words to sting a little, but

was astonished at the extent of their effect when her father, without another word, turned and left the room, leaving her in ignorance of whether he was grieved or angry.

But at least he had given her plenty to think about. She could not now any longer refuse to consider the question of what Geoffrey's meaning might be. It was evident that she would not be allowed to keep him only as a friend, her father did not understand such friendships. The frank, good-fellowship which he had allowed between Bernard Offord and the girls had been very different, he had been companion to them all until just before leaving for India, when he had fancied himself in love with Adelaide, and she had laughed at him, but there was nothing in Geoffrey's character or behaviour resembling this. In her father's eyes he must be her suitor or nothing; and although she was satisfied, for she believed that he loved her, she could not say so until he had told her.

It was cruel to take away from her, without reason, the one pleasure of receiving his letters, for he told her in this first one that he meant to write from time to time; she was not sure that she should not rebel. She had been left to herself so long that she almost felt a right to her own way, and she believed that when she told Geoffrey of her father's objection he would agree with her that it was unreasonable, and need not be altogether binding. It was true that since her accident her father had been kind to her whenever they were together, but it was in his nature to be kind to anything which he fancied weak or suffering, and he had left it to a stranger to discover first that his slighted daughter had something to recommend her after all. No, she could not feel that these few tokens of pity, rather than love, were more than a feather weight in the scale against those long years of neglect and misconception.

But yet she was sorry, very sorry, that just when it seemed possible that a better understanding was beginning, a more serious difference than had ever before arisen should come between them.

She could not explain the matter to Geoffrey and ask his advice, but she believed that almost at a word he would understand the state of the case, and whatever he told her she would do, even if he decided that she owed to her father an obedience which she neither regarded as a duty nor wished to show. She understood that she had been forbidden to answer this letter, but this command she should certainly disobey; Geoffrey should not think her ungrateful or careless, but how she should learn what he thought of the matter she did not know, for she could not for a moment suppose that her father would allow her to receive another letter from him. It would have been better after all if she had died out there in the long, cold night, instead of coming back again to a life where no one wanted her, excepting the one friend who was forbidden.

It was a great effort to go down when the luncheon-bell rang, but she scarcely dared to disregard it, and her silence was nothing unusual; but her surprise was almost over-powering when, as she was leaving the table, again her father called her back, and said quietly, but in a tone of displeasure—

"You had better answer the letter which Mr. Poland has written you, Laura, and tell him that I do not approve of any further correspondence. You can put yours into this envelope with mine, which I wish you to read, before you post it, at your leisure.

Laura took the letter in silence, and left the room.

She had no notion what to say, and the unexpected leniency was more difficult to deal with than the sternest rebuke. It cut away the ground under her feet, and she could no longer feel herself a victim of tyranny, when the disobedience she had meditated was turned into a permitted indulgence.

She went back to the blue study and sat there a long while, seeing nothing of the fair sunny sky and breeze-blown trees through the open window, while the letter lay unopened in her lap. Was it after all her father's duty to refuse her this coveted pleasure? He had no cause to trust Geoffrey as she did, with all her heart—believing that if he loved her well enough he would before long come back and take her, and if not—well! they could be faithful friends through all their lives, if only other people—well-meaning, perhaps—would keep silence and leave them alone.

She could not write her letter that day, she must take long to think over it, and she shrank a little from seeing what her father had written, and yet her words must be guided by his. She could not pour out her thoughts to her friend if her father had said anything which could lower her in his eyes. Well! She would read that first, and then give her whole mind to pondering over what this one only letter she might write should contain.

"DEAR POLAND," Mr. Hilton wrote, "I am most glad to hear that your health is entirely restored, and that you have good prospect of occupation, which is so necessary for every one, especially for a man of your age. You may be sure that we shall always hear of you with interest. I have given your note to my daughter, and desired her to answer it, but I have also told her that I should tell you that I do not approve of further correspondence. We shall hope to hear of your welfare through Mrs. Mathewson.

"Faithfully yours,
"WEDGWOOD HILTON."

Laura gave a sigh of relief. There was nothing there to wound her, although there was no encouragement to further intercourse, and indeed scarcely a loophole. Then she put on her hat and went out into the sunshine, and wandered up to the Lookout, and sat there gazing out over the fair, wide scene, with almost unconscious eyes until the sinking sun warned her to return.

CHAPTER XVIII.

THE SECOND LETTER.

LIFE went on very quietly at Blithefield in Edith's absence. Mr. Hilton did not care for society when she was not there to take all the trouble of it off his shoulders, and leave him free to see as much or as little of any one as he pleased, and visitors found that although Mary and Erica were pleasant additions when Edith was there, yet without her as the centre the house did not seem at all like itself.

Laura was desired by her father to take her place at the head of the table, but there her duties began and ended, excepting every now and then, when an invitation was so worded that it could not be accepted without her, and her father insisted on her going with the others.

Mrs. Paget and Mrs. Bonar offered to take it in turns to stay at Blithefield while their sister was away, but Mr. Hilton would not hear of it. It would be at the sacrifice of the comfort of their own homes, and he could not allow it, and "thanks to Miss Verney" they could get on very well, and he would not even openly confess in his letters to Edith that he missed her, although she could see it in every line he wrote. Well, two months was not a very long time, and when the weather was fine he could be out a great deal, and could drive Mary and Erica all over the country with his favourite grays. About a fortnight after Geoffrey Poland's first letter, Mr. Hilton received another one from him, but as it was lying underneath some others on the

breakfast table he supposed that none of
the girls had seen it, and put it in his
pocket to read quietly in his study.

He was curious to see what it contained,
for he could imagine no reason for Geoffrey's
writing again, and Edith had told him
several times that he neither inquired after
any one at Blithefield, nor appeared to take
an interest in the home news which she
often discussed with Mrs. Mathewson at
breakfast time She tried to be a good
sister, and considerate friend, and always
spoke of Laura when she could find
occasion, and she was vexed that her father
had forbidden the correspondence, and told
him so; but he only smiled to himself as he
read and thought—" Of course, one girl
would stick up for another in a thing like
that, and even Edith's wise little head was
not quite so strong as her heart." He was
rather absent during breakfast time, and

cast many glances at Laura, taking but little notice of Erica's chatter, which Mary, seeing that he was preoccupied, tried as far as possible to direct to herself.

Perhaps, he thought to himself, he had done just the wisest thing in forbidding them to write, and had hurried on the desirable climax in the most judicious manner; if so, who could say again that a father did not know how to manage for his girls? He cut the usual discussion of plans for the day very short, saying that he had letters to attend to just then, and hurrying to his study opened the envelope, which contained a fastened but unaddressed enclosure.

" Dear Sir," Geoffrey wrote, " I regret that you should object to an occasional correspondence between your daughter and myself. It would have been a pleasure to both of us, and we have many interests in common; but I must, of course, bow to your wishes. I will, however, ask you to do me the favour of allowing her to receive this one more note which I inclose, giving her information on some points which we discussed together. If you object to her receiving it, I request you to direct it back to me, which will save you the trouble of writing.

"Yours faithfully,

"GEOFFREY POLAND."

Mr. Hilton felt thoroughly angry and perplexed. "A bit of confounded impudence on Poland's part," he considered this request, and it put him in a most uncomfortable position. After the unpleasant scene which he had had with Laura a few days before, he was anxious to avoid further discussion with her, and yet he considered that his position as her father demanded that this breach of the rule that he had made should not be passed over without remark. Of course the easiest thing for himself would be to send the letter back and say nothing to Laura about it; but this would be hard upon her, and he did not wish to be hard, only to protect her against her own inexperience and Geoffrey's possible trifling. If "the fellow" really cared for her he would only put a higher value upon her from having a few difficulties thrown in his way, and if he had any sense he would understand from the words which had passed between them at parting, that when he chose to come again he would be welcome.

Well! there seemed only one thing to be done, give Laura her choice of having her letter after he had read it, or of its being sent back unopened, and he could not doubt that she would choose the first alternative, for he had distinctly understood from her that there was no sort of understanding between them which would entitle Geoffrey to write her a love-letter. He was disappointed, and tried to believe that it was for her sake, but, in truth, the management of this daughter had become too much for him.

Once more he went to seek her in the blue study. It was a wet chilly morning and although May was almost at an end, he found her sitting by a bright little fire, with books and papers spread out on a table beside her, while her embroidery frame was pushed back into a corner. She rose hastily, gathering her things together in confusion as her father came in, but he was too much occupied with his own thoughts to notice her.

" Laura, I have heard again from Poland this morning," he said abruptly. She said nothing, but changed colour a little, and waited for him to go on.

"He has asked me to give you another note from him, but, of course, I cannot do so without reading it, as I told him I did not approve of his writing to you."

As he spoke he laid the letter on the table. Laura was silent for a moment, then she said resolutely—

"I should very much object to your reading Mr. Poland's letter, father."

"I am sorry to hear it, for it proves that they are not suitable for you to receive."

"No, father, it does not prove that, it only shows that he and I have thoughts in which you could not share, and which neither of us would wish to discuss with you." She was trying hard to speak sensibly and temperately, and was surprised to find that she had only succeeded in making him angry.

"I wonder you are not ashamed to confess it to me," he exclaimed. "You cannot imagine that I should allow any sort of intercourse if the thoughts which this man puts into your mind or fosters there are not fit to come to my knowledge. I shall certainly read this letter, and if——" but before he finished speaking, Laura snatched it from the table and flung it into the briskly blazing fire, then with a white face she turned round and tried to speak, but words would not come, and she hurried from the room before he could recover from his surprise.

It was not often that Mr. Hilton used strong language, but a few forcible words were a necessary relief when he found himself alone, and hot and angry he hastened back to his study and shut the door, with a noisy violence which startled Erica from her practising in the room above.

Had any man ever before been cursed with such a daughter? he wondered in his first anger. A daughter with such an abominable temper, such unbounded insolence, and such ingenuity in making herself odious?

All the kindness he had lately felt towards her vanished again in this wrathful moment, and he felt that his only desire was to get rid of her; and yet she had shown him lately, and had brought it home to him, that her faults were due as much to his neglect as to her own failings. Plain, perverse, uninteresting; truly all these she had been from babyhood; but it was a terrible, almost an unheard-of, misfortune that neither father nor mother should have been able to love her in spite of it all. A childhood without love! —it needed, indeed, a sweet and rare nature to pass through it unwarped. But it was too late to repent of all that now, and, at

least through all her life, she had had exam-
ples before her of unfailing good temper and
unbroken affection amongst her sisters, who
almost seemed to be made of different flesh
and blood from herself.

It was hard enough at any time for a man
to be left with five motherless girls on his
hands, but when one of them was possessed
with a demon of perversity, the hand of misfortune pressed heavily indeed.

Then, when he had calmed down a little,
it was the awkwardness of his own position
which struck him most forcibly.   What
could he say to Poland? how account for
neither delivering his letter nor sending it
back?   He certainly had no wish to adver-
tise his daughter's ill-temper by describing
exactly what had happened; for although he
would not, of course, wish any man to marry
her in ignorance of her faults, it would only
be a straining of honesty to allude to such a

scene as that just past. How much he wished that Edith was there to talk it over with him, and suggest some means "of getting out of the mess" with dignity, and without compromising Laura, and still more to soothe the pangs of self-reproach for past neglect which hurt in proportion to their truth! Well, he must think the matter over, and would do nothing until the next day; but whatever happened, he would take care not to let Poland think that in any way he had got the better of him.

Then it suddenly struck him that he would ride over and tell Janet all about it. She was a "comfortable" daughter in any perplexity, and although she had never seen Poland, she understood pretty well how the land lay. So he rang the bell and ordered his horse, and then found Mary and Erica in the garden, and told them not to expect him until dinner time, thus doing away with the necessity of encountering his rebellious daughter for some hours.

Erica had guessed that there was something wrong when she saw her father go up to the blue study, and had afterwards heard the violent shutting of his own door; but although intensely curious, she scarcely dared to ask any questions, feeling sure that the difficulty must be a big one, as he was apparently going to consult over it with Janet.

"I *do* wonder what it is, Mary," she said, when he had ridden away.. "There was certainly some important letter this morning, and it must be about Mr. Poland, if it is anything to do with Laura."

"Yes, very likely; but I think we had better not talk about it, Erica," answered Mary. "Your father is evidently in anxiety, and perhaps Laura is in trouble; but I don't think even you are meant to interfere, and we must just try to seem unconscious, and keep the house as bright as we can."

"Oh, Mary you are so wise and good," sighed Erica; "but you don't understand that dear old father, generally, lets us say and do what we please, and if he had stayed another minute I should have screwed up my courage, and asked him what it was all about."

"I am glad you did not, I am sure it would have worried him, and he did not look as if he could bear much more just then. Now let us get as far as the river and back before the luncheon-bell rings."

Erica felt a little offended, but was too good-tempered to let it last long; but there was a triumphant, "I told you so!" in her look when Stephens brought a message to say that "Miss Laura was not coming down to luncheon."

"Poor Laura! I am sorry for her," said

Mary when they were alone, "but I am afraid neither you nor I could do any good by interfering."

"Not I, certainly," answered Erica, carelessly. "She would burn or freeze me with a look the moment I went into the room. She is quite sure not to appear this afternoon, so let us drive the ponies over to Adelaide's, and play tennis with Edgar."

And Mary reluctantly consented, not seeing that she could do any good by staying at home.

Mr. Hilton on reaching Daisy Lodge felt still more deeply plunged into misfortune, when he found that Janet had taken her nurse and children to spend the day with a friend. Captain Bonar was at home, busy amongst his flower beds, but of course the subject could not be mentioned to him, and after having his luncheon Mr. Hilton resolved to ride on and see Adelaide, whose advice was sure to be sound and good, if not so shrewd as Janet's. But scarcely had he reached the pretty rectory before the pony carriage with Mary and Erica drove up, and his second chance was gone.

Mr. Paget was out, so there was no tennis to occupy the girls, and as Mr. Hilton was particularly anxious that Erica should know nothing of the matter, he could not suggest that he wished for a private conversation with Adelaide, and could only fall in with Erica's suggestion that as they had driven over alone—which was rather against his rules—he should ride beside the pony carriage and take care of them going home. He tried to forget his troubles, in playing with his little grandsons, with whom he was a great favourite, and had so far succeeded as to be in the middle of telling them a story, when Adelaide's question—"Why did not Laura come this afternoon?" and Erica's answer: "Oh, she had a headache or something, and did not come down to luncheon" — put all his ideas to flight.

Erica, too, had looked keenly at him when she spoke, as if she suspected something; and feeling thoroughly put out, he made an excuse of being tired, and had his horse brought round, leaving the girls to follow at their leisure.

"You look worried, father dear," said Adelaide anxiously, when she had followed him to the gate, while the others remained on the lawn.

"Yes, I am in difficulty, Adelaide, and came to speak to you about it, but I have not had a chance. It is about Laura and that fellow, Poland; but I don't wish Erica to know anything about it."

"Could you not stop and tell me now, father?"

"No, my dear, she would see that there was something wrong, and set her quick wits to find out what it was.; and although Laura has been much to blame, I do not want the whole world to know it. I must just make my way out of it as best I can."

"Shall I come over to-morrow and see what I can do?"

"Yes, I wish you would, but I must lose no time in deciding what line I mean to take;" and then he rode away, feeling that his attempts to shift his burden a little had been very unsuccessful.

When he got home he went straight to his study, and found lying on his desk an undirected letter. He opened it in surprise, and found a few lines from Laura, enclosing another sheet.

"Since you went out," she wrote, "I have

written and posted a letter to Mr. Poland, of which I inclose a copy for you to read. I want him to know why I destroyed his letter without knowing a word of its contents.

"LAURA."

These few lines brought Mr. Hilton instant, although only partial, relief. It was an abominable piece of disobedience on her part to write to the fellow again after she had been forbidden, but it removed from him the difficulty of explaining why the letter was neither delivered nor sent back, and although it must make him appear as a tyrant, he did not particularly care for that. It was clearly his duty, although a distasteful one, to read the letter Laura had written, and learn on what footing she had placed herself. It was very short, but it both grieved and angered him :—

" DEAR GEOFFREY,—My father brought me

a note from you this morning, but he would not allow me to have it without reading it himself first, and to this I could not consent. I believe you will think me right in that; but I must confess to you that I lost my temper over it and threw the letter unopened into the fire, so I shall never have the least idea of what you had written. You will know that it grieved me. There will be no use in your writing again; I shall not be allowed to receive a letter from you. I am doing many of the things we talked about, and hope in time to do more.

" Your faithful friend,

" LAURA HILTON."

" Poor child ! poor child ! " said her father, when he laid it down; " but I am doing what is right for her against her will, and giving him a chance of proving of what metal he is made."

CHAPTER XIX.

A TRUCE.

But although Mr. Hilton felt much pity for his daughter, it was impossible that he could altogether pass over her disobedience and undutifulness. She had saved him from the difficulty of an explanation with Geoffrey, and he felt secretly grateful to her; but if he allowed her to think that she could take matters into her own hands in this fashion, there was no knowing to what length she might go. Thus he found it absurdly difficult to decide what to say to her. She could no longer be treated like a child, and threatened with punishment, and he had no reason to suppose that a few severe words—

which would have made Edith miserable
and repentant, and dissolved Erica into
tears—would have any effect upon her; it
would need love to give point to the words,
and there was little enough of that between
them. Of course there was a sort of root
of affection for each other in their hearts,
from which on special occasions sprang a
forced and hasty blossom of emotion, but it
scarcely bore the light of common day, and
faded and drooped in an hour.

The whole thing was a horrible nuisance,
and he wished that it was consistent with
his position to say no more about it; but it
was clearly his duty to watch over his
daughter against her will, and he had no
intention of shirking it, although by the
time the dinner-bell rang he had made up
his mind to say nothing until the next
morning.

In the meantime, Laura—although she

did not repent—was much frightened at what she had done. It was bad enough to have burnt the letter, but to have deliberately disobeyed her father by writing again was, of course, infinitely worse. She did not deserve kindness from him now, she knew that well, but then there were—oh such long arrears of neglect to be paid! that from her point of view, although, of course, not from his, she felt that she owed him little obedience.

It was impossible that she should appear before him without his leave, he *must* be deeply angry with her, and although she could not tell him that she was sorry for what she had done, she could and would show him the respect of acknowledging that she was in disgrace. So when the dinner-bell rang she sent a message to say that she hoped he would excuse her from coming down that evening, and Mr. Hilton took his

place at the dinner-table with Mary and
Erica with a considerable lightening of his
spirits, feeling relieved and cheerful. There
was a great deal in not having the culprit
before his eyes to remind him that he had
before him the detestable necessity of finding
fault with her again, and the girls, knowing
that he had been worried, exerted themselves
to amuse him with such good effect that
more than half Laura's self-reproach would
have vanished if she had seen how completely
he seemed to forget her, her faults, and her
troubles, while she, stealing out quietly in
the dusk, paced up and down the garden
paths, thinking what a different world it was
to her from that of a year ago, and how
far more different it might be if people were
allowed to harmlessly shape their lives
according to their own pattern.

Mr. Hilton generally went to his study to
smoke after prayers at ten o'clock, but this

evening Mary and Erica succeeded so well in banishing, for the time, his unpleasant thoughts, that it was nearly eleven before he wished them good night, and he had scarcely had time to settle himself comfortably in front of the fire, when, after a quiet knock, Laura came in, looking pale and tired, and still in her morning dress, and stood at a little distance from him, nervously grasping the back of a chair.

"I have come to ask you whether you intend to forgive me, father?" she said. "I supposed you would wish me to keep out of your sight until you gave me leave to do as usual, but uncertainty is so miserable! And I could not sleep until I had asked you whether you will allow me to come down to breakfast to-morrow?"

"Of course! of course!" answered her father, hurriedly, taken uncomfortably by surprise, and not in the least knowing what to say. "I never thought of your staying upstairs; but, of course, you know that it must be understood that this sort of thing will not happen again?"

"Yes, I suppose so," answered Laura, wearily, "but I don't want to deceive you father, and I had better tell you plainly that I cannot make any promises. I think it is quite impossible that we should understand each other, but I will do my best to obey you, only I *must* tell you that occasions may arise when I shall feel a right to judge for myself."

"That is all nonsense! You cannot possibly have a right to put your judgment before mine. But I think you are making yourself out to be a good deal worse than you need. You let your temper get the better of you and acted very wrongly to-day; but you have confessed your fault, and I am willing to forgive it, and say no more about it."

He felt that he was acting weakly, and scarcely doing his duty by his daughter, at least not that strict duty which had made him interfere about Geoffrey's letters; but he was heartily sick of the whole business, and only too glad of any loophole for escape from further discussion. It was not likely that Poland would presume to write again, or that Laura would volunteer any communication with him; and as he was far from wishing either of them to think that he should disapprove of Geoffrey as a *bonâ fide* suitor, it would probably be wisest to say no more about him until he chose to appear again.

Laura felt relieved by her father's manner, but yet it jarred upon her that he should seem to treat so lightly now a matter of such importance to her. If he really did not care much about it, why had he interfered at all? She had supposed that he did it from a sense of duty, and she had felt respect for his opinion; but if he cared so little it could be scarcely more than a caprice, and one that only pushed her to a further distance from him.

She stood for a minute or two, waiting for him to speak again; and at last he looked up and said with the involuntary sharpness of extreme discomfort—

"You need not wait, Laura, unless you have anything more you wish to say."

And she left him without another word, with tears in her eyes, but hurt and angry, and feeling that the distance between them could hardly be greater than she should wish.

When Mrs. Paget came the next morning —full of sympathy with her father, and prepared to act as mediator—he felt a little awkward. He had certainly made too much of the matter the day before, and regretted it now; and when Adelaide kissed him with effusion, and said sympathetically, "I hope you feel better to-day, dear father?" he answered, almost impatiently—

"Oh, yes, thank you, my dear; I am all right this morning. There is nothing like sleeping over a difficulty, and Laura and I have had a little explanation, and things will go on as usual."

"You do not wish me to speak to her on the subject, then?" asked Adelaide with some disappointment. She had half hoped that on this occasion Laura might open her heart to her.

"No, I think you had better say nothing about it to any one; we understand each other pretty well now, and I hope we shall have no more difficulties."

So there was nothing for Adelaide to do but to be rather kinder to Laura than usual, and to parry Erica's questions, who, knowing that something was wrong, and that she was being purposely kept in the dark, felt unbounded curiosity.

" It was horrid of father, and not a-bit like him!" she said; " but she supposed that, having seen more of Laura lately, he had learned from her to be disagreeable;" and she was additionally hurt from imagining, what was indeed the truth, that Mary knew a great deal more about it all than she did, for Adelaide felt a necessity for talking to some one, and allowed herself to speak as openly to Mary as she would have done to Edith if she had been at home.

Although supposed to take little heed of what went on around her, Laura perceived that the household was sitting in judgment upon her, and feeling unable either to ignore

it or treat it with the contempt that she
would have wished, she asked for the use of
the pony carriage to drive to Daisy Lodge,
and see Janet and the babies. But even
then she was not allowed to escape observation altogether, for Morris, who was driving
her, pulled up the ponies at a certain point,
and said with an air of being sure of interesting her—

"Beg pardon, miss, but 'twas just here
that Mr. Poland stood up and waved his hat
that morning you come by your accident.
'Pull up a-bit, Morris,' says he, and I felt
put about like, not knowing what he was
after, but I s'pose he knew you was there,
miss?"

"Yes, Morris," answered Laura, feeling
that he did not intend any liberty, and that
to deny it would be foolish.

"And then he says, 'You can see a good
bit of the road from that hill there in the

Park, can't you?' meaning the Look-out, miss, and I says, 'Yes, sir, you can,' and he sits down, quite contented like, and I never gave it a thought that he meant you was there, miss."

"No, Morris, of course not," answered Laura quietly, and her manner gave no further opening for remarks.

A few days later Laura handed to her father a letter she had received from Edith, giving a pleasant account of what she was seeing and doing, but with a postscript which was evidently the cause of its being written. "Mr. Poland has just come in," she said, "and has asked me to thank you for your last note, and to say that he thoroughly understands it."

Mr. Hilton gave back the letter without remark, but with a cordial, "Thank you, my dear," and a kind smile, which showed Laura that the effort she had made in showing it to him was appreciated; but it was with a heavy sigh that she went back to the blue study, and tried to give her whole attention to books, which she was slowly learning to love, first for Geoffrey's sake, and then for their own.

END OF VOL. I.

www.ingramcontent.com/pod-product-compliance
Lightning Source LLC
Chambersburg PA
CBHW020848020726
47497CB00005B/1313